mage of mango road

DEAD & BREAKFAST #3

GABRIELLE KEYES

ALIENHEAD PRESS

ASIN: B09LH8XXLT (EBOOK EDITION)

ISBN: 9798433372207 (Paperback)

PRINTED AND BOUND IN THE UNITED STATES OF AMERICA

FIRST PRINTING MARCH 2022

PUBLISHED BY ALIENHEAD PRESS

MIAMI, FL 33186

mage of mango road

For my family

* * *

There is freedom waiting for you
On the breezes of the sky.
And you ask,
"What if I fall?"
Oh, but my darling . . . what if you fly?

- ERIN HANSON

* * *

one

I WAS DROWNING AGAIN.

Sinking in turquoise waters. Watching the sun on the oxygenated side of the surface get smaller and smaller, as I sank deeper in the wrong direction. Arms flailing. Legs pumping. Lungs burning.

Why weren't they coming after me? No one saw me fall in? They fussed over me constantly, but now when it mattered, no one noticed me plummeting? Into the depths. I couldn't breathe. Couldn't cry. Couldn't hear voices.

The silence was deafening.

The ocean squeezed my tiny body.

It was dark when my soul detached, debating whether it should leave. But then someone was there—an angel in the depths. Pushing me upwards. Nudging. Poking. Upwards. Toward the surface, small bursts at a time, gliding me back to the world of the living. Burst...float...burst.

Upwards, upwards. Suspended in darkness, pressure all around, but soon that pressure lightened. Almost there. Almost to the surface. Each time I dreamed this, I saw the sun-broiled arms reaching down, puncturing the water's surface, heard people shouting orders, felt sharp edges of wooden raft scrape my forehead, as my angel rescuer pushed me up and out of the sea into the summer air. A man's hand clasped my arm, tugging, saving me.

But then—

I slipped out of his grasp back into the ocean once again. Greedy ocean. Only this time, there were no angels to save me. I was alone again. Sinking, sinking, down into another realm...

...and the world went dark.

I shot out of bed, gasping for air. Hands at my throat. Shaking. Unfamiliar surroundings. Waves lapping against the shore outside an open window. Soft breezes blowing in. I was above water. On land.

Not drowning.

Not drowning.

Relax, Reggie. It's the same old dream.

I glanced around, panting. Early morning light leaked into my barely furnished room. I dropped my sweaty face into my hands and sobbed, panic and fear leaking from my brain into my fingertips. Stupid dream. Stupid, stupid dream. I flung off the comforter and checked the time.

Time to get up, that's what.

Even in rest, I couldn't rest.

New place. New job.

It was my third day working for a lady named Lily Autumn in a place called *Dead & Breakfast*, and there was so much weirdness here, my husband would've made me quit had he seen it. Creepy dolls at the Berry House, witchy things at the Jackson House. Here at Montero House, the place had no theme yet; they were still in the early stages of renovating. At least I had a paycheck coming, and it was a free place to stay.

After Daniel died, I couldn't afford the apartment by myself, so I moved in with our son, Andreas, and my daughter-in-law, Melinda, for six months. It didn't take a genius, however, to realize I was intruding on their lives, that having Mom around wasn't a good mood setter for baby-making. And because I never intended to be a burden on anyone, I started looking for a new place to live, but couldn't find anything with my slim earnings.

Andreas suggested I move in with Cici, my never-married, never-had-kids elderly sister-in-law, and while my son was good with the thought of two older ladies taking care of each other, absolving him of the responsibility, I was not. I'd rather clean houses the rest of my life and try for a place of my own than share a pee-smelling apartment with a spinster and her three yapping dogs.

But then, my cousin who worked at a TV station in Miami told me about this job in the islands. On a whim, I applied. On a whim, they hired me. Now, here I was—the saddest woman in paradise.

I threw on my apron and headed downstairs into the disarray of the Montero House. I wouldn't be working here, just sleeping. Ms. Lily gave me the option of living here temporarily or staying at a nearby motel while the house was getting renovated. "Also," she'd said during the interview, "you should know it's reputably haunted." She made air quotes with her fingers.

I didn't have a problem with haunted. I'd lived in a haunted house all my life, but my family never liked for me to talk about that. "I'll take the Montero House," I'd replied easily. The house felt like it was leaning and had been gutted top to bottom, except for my bedroom and bathroom. There was 1980s paneling, carpeting, and cabinetry outside in portable dumpsters by the street, but still, it was a beautiful Southern home.

With a monkey sitting on the front porch.

I gasped. Its little brown eyes stared at me, cream-colored fur fluffed in the breeze, dexterous little hands wrapped around something in its lap.

"Hi?" I twiddled my fingers.

He chirped, cocked his head, and handed me something —a small, underripe green mango.

"Uh, thank you." I took it. It was too hard to eat. I smiled at him. "I'll eat it later. Thank you again."

He must've been offended that I wouldn't eat it now, because he chirped, threw a mangrove seed pod at me, then scurried into the dense vegetation.

"Sorry. It's just not ready to eat yet!" I called. "Aaaandd... I'm apologizing to a monkey."

I set the mango on the floor inside the front door and closed both the door and screen. With a deep breath, I set out on my morning walk to *House of Dolls*, the second *Dead & Breakfast* belonging to celebrity chef, Lily Autumn.

As always, I used my walk to work as time to thank God for allowing me to greet a new day, even if my husband and younger son, Pablito, hadn't been as lucky, even if my life had been fraught with struggle. I tried to focus on the positive, to remember that I was blessed, but it wasn't easy.

I missed my son.

Daniel's death had been expected, but a young, healthy twenty-five-year-old? A mother should never have to bury her child—ever—in any universe. I'd go crazy if I thought about it too much. Still, I'd been fortunate in other ways: Daniel's family had taken me in when I washed ashore long ago, and I had this job. Sure, its location was a mere two hundred miles from Cuba, a country my parents had fled, risking death at sea in order to give me life, but my checking account was no longer overdrawn.

I tried not to focus on the fact that taking this position felt, at times, like ten steps in the wrong direction. Northward, away from Cuba, meant freedom. Southward meant back to my starting point, like falling back into the ocean. Also, no little girl dreams of cleaning houses when she grows up, of being the "cinder" part of Cinderella, but I had no other choice.

And...as far as employers went, Lily Autumn was a breath of fresh air. You might know her as the host of *Witch of Key Lime Lane*. Everybody else did. I had no clue; I didn't have cable, Netflix, or any TV for that matter. My very limited me-time was all about reading—history, travel, a little science fiction—but Lily was hiring, and according to my cousin, the woman helped changed people's lives.

At first, I was scared of her. Her reputation included a well-known incident wherein she burned her ex-husband's things in a bonfire after she found out he was cheating. But when I met her in person, she was nothing like I'd imagined —confident, independent, talented, bright, positive, full of skills and traits I simply did not have. Most employers wanted to know if I had a criminal background.

Lily wanted to know: "Tell me, Regina, what are your dreams?"

"My dreams?" I'd given her a long, blank stare.

What dreams?

She honestly thought I had ambition outside of coping with the deaths of my son and husband? It'd been so long since I even *thought* about dreams that it felt like she was referring to fairytales and castles in lands far, far away.

I made something up. "I've always wanted to run a store of my own."

"Oh, nice! What kind of store?" Her hazel eyes had lit up with interest.

"Umm, any store?"

Any store. I could've slapped myself. *Way to show true grit and determination, Reg!*

Now that I'd had some time to think about it, what I'd meant was—I wanted freedom. The type of store didn't matter. What I wanted was what *she* had—the independence to work in a place of *my* own, open it with *my* key, work for *my*self. To never again worry whether I'd meet rent that month. To never again clean another toilet that wasn't mine.

Imagine my shock when she'd smiled wistfully then hired me anyway. I'd like to think she saw something in me.

I climbed up to *House of Dolls*, the tall purple bed-and-breakfast with the black shutters and spider web gates. A more beautiful creepy dollhouse I never did see. Except for the other one I cleaned—*Sylvie & Lily's Dead & Breakfast* over on Key Lime Lane. Yesterday, I made all the renovated rooms sparkle, including the new theater entrance hall. Talk about ornate, gothic Victorian! My task for today? To get the kitchen and dining areas ready for its first guests.

For hours, I unboxed stemware and dinnerware with delicate doll silhouettes on them, polished wooden tables, and swept new hardwood floors. The neighbor, Nanette, made me coffee (though I didn't drink it), her grandson, Sam, showed me amazing illustrations on his tablet, and the contractor of the renovation, a man so very easy on the eyes named Evan, flashed me a smile from the front porch.

Was something going on?

A lively energy buzzed through the house that I couldn't quite put my finger on. I'd just stacked an assortment of creepy mugs, sugar packets, and spoons that looked like skulls when a tall woman, wearing a sleeveless, purple dress and black boots, black hair cut to her shoulder with a ribbon of silver snaking through it, and bright red lips, walked in. She lowered her shades and grinned at me.

I stared.

She studied me for the briefest of moments before leaping into the arms of the super handsome contractor who snuck up behind her. Watching them canoodle, I wondered if anyone would ever hug me that way again. I closed my mouth before it caught flies and entered the kitchen, sidling up to another girl hired last week. As she straightened kitchen towels, I leaned in. "Do you know who that is?" I gestured to the purple dress lady.

The Cher-when-she-was-young housekeeper looked at me like I had three heads. "That's Katja Miller."

"Who?"

"The new host of the spinoff they're about to start taping? *Crone of Coconut Court?*" She almost scoffed.

"Oh." Was I supposed to know her?

Talk of TV shows was the easiest, quickest way to lose

7

me. If anyone ever wanted to rid the room of Regina Serra, all they needed to do was mention the newest, hottest TV show.

The nowhere-near "crone" was full of confidence I'd never have, not even if they gave it away for free at the dollar store. I'd find some way of losing it. Women like Katja were born that way. They received a self-assurance gene at conception that had unfortunately escaped me. They knew the right hairstyles, the right colors to wear, how to do cat-wing eyeliner. They carried their bodies in a way that said I'M THE BOSS.

All my body language said was I WISH.

I wish I could walk into a room like I owned it. I wish this house was mine. I wish I'd done more with my life.

Wishing was a timewaster. *Back to work.* Through the kitchen window, I spotted Ms. Lily, in khaki shorts, a pretty boho top, and leather brown sandals, coming up the steps. Trotting alongside her was a beautiful gray kitty.

I carried a large crystal vase sprouting dozens of burnt orange sunflowers back to the dining hall, crossing the foyer just as Lily walked through the door.

"Well? Where is she?" she asked.

"Katja Miller?" I peeked through the sunflowers. "She went through those doors over there." With my chin, I gestured at the adjacent theater. "I'll go get her for you."

"Not her," Lily chirped, taking the vase from my hands and setting them on the dining table. She whirled around. "You! How are you doing? I haven't seen you since your interview. Are you good? Do you need anything? Can I make your stay more comfortable in any way?"

"Oh, um, I'm great! Thank you...so much?"

For asking.

She squeezed my arms, as I stood there, trying to remember if any employer had ever been so kind as to ask me how I was doing and mean it. I might've been to hell and back the last few years. I might've had a rocky start to life. I might've had bad dreams every other night, and I might've suffered from survivor's guilt and an embarrassing case of low self-esteem, but I was here. In Skeleton Key. Surrounded by nice people.

Could've been worse.

A little girl in an old-timey dress giggled at me from the stairwell. She was not doing a very good job of hiding. I smiled at her. Her mother, in a bright yellow dress with a bow at her waist, told her to come along and leave me alone. I watched the two of them float down the stairs and disappear through a wall, like I'd seen thousands of ghosts do since the day I was pulled lifeless aboard a raft at the age of three.

I wish I could start a new life.

Like I did the day I was rescued at sea.

But that kind of luck doesn't happen twice.

two

THAT NIGHT, trying to fall asleep, I stared at the old popcorn ceiling a long time. I listened to waves lapping softly against the shore. It was February in South Florida, which meant windows could stay open without residents melting into the floor.

I'd had quite a day, beginning with the awful dream, having a monkey get mad at me, meeting two TV show hosts and two ghosts at the place where I worked, but despite this (or maybe because of it), I still couldn't turn off my brain. That seemed to be happening a lot these days, and everyone I knew seemed to have an opinion about it.

It's perimenopause.

It's grief.

It's stress.

It's menopause.

It's your thyroid.

It's lack of Vitamin D.

It's exhaustion.

How about: *it's all of the above.*

Not to mention another strange phenomenon no one knew about but me—the closer to my birth country I happened to be, the more intense my drowning dreams, as though Cuba were the epicenter of my emotional pain radar. Also, the closer to water I happened to be, the more my "sight" intensified. I hadn't seen ghosts in a while, yet today I'd seen two.

I didn't mind the ghosts, but people didn't like to hear about them, so I'd learned early on in life not to talk about them. Growing up in Daniel's parents' house, I'd seen plenty of dead family members, but his grandmother was Catholic and didn't like the idea that loved ones, who by all accounts should've made it to the kingdom of Heaven, were roaming the hallways in our Westchester house. I tried explaining how we're made of dense material (bodies) and light energetic material (souls), and how, when we die, it's just the dense material that withers—the rest of us sticks around.

"Ghosts are normal, Abuela," I'd tried explaining to my grandmother once, "It's not that different from the Father, the Son, and the Holy Spirit, except it's Cuco, Lela, and Tío Pepe watching you when you sleep."

That did not go over well.

Over time, I learned to suppress my abilities. Daniel's family were my world, my rescuers, and I didn't want to offend them. His parents took me in after my own died during a dangerous pilgrimage from Cuba to the United States called the Mariel Boat Lift. I survived, and his folks, who were friends of my parents and their parents' parents from back in the old country, adopted me. Raised me as their own. That's how Daniel and I grew up together in the same house. Everyone always said we would get married one day.

Well, we did.

And God forgive me for saying so, but it was akin to marrying a stepbrother or a cousin with the way we knew everything about each other. Too close. Too familiar. But hindsight is 20/20 and there was nothing to be done about it now. Six months ago, Daniel left us after a brief battle with Stage 4 pancreatic cancer, three years to the day that our son Pablito was killed in a hit-and-run DUI. After that, I was left with little to call my own, except for Andreas, now married. We never had much to begin with. We came from a humble, religious upbringing that saw hard work, childrearing, and poverty as virtues.

The ceiling hadn't changed much after an hour of staring at it. Eventually, I drifted off to sleep, but it wasn't long before normal brainwave activity morphed into fresh, vividly lucid dreams again. I was outside this house, facing the Atlantic Ocean. Sunny day. Brilliant, white light. Gorgeous blue sky. Not hot at all, just pleasant temperature. I was sitting on the sand, staring out at the ocean. While I did not like being on the water, I didn't mind looking at it.

That was when a rugged, older man, bronzed from years in the sun, came walking down the beach wearing dark pants from before my time and a blue guayabera shirt with a straw hat. *Hello?* I said. His face was partially covered by the hat, and I hadn't been on this island long enough to know anyone who lived here.

What are you working towards? the man asked.

Towards? I don't work towards anything. I work to survive.

I wanted to argue that it was all downhill from here, but the man seemed sincere in his question to me; I didn't want to be rude.

What does it all mean? Make it mean something.

Excuse me? He didn't know me. He didn't know my pain. He didn't know that my chance to make work "mean something" was over. That I'd sacrificed my good years in support of a man who'd left his wife with little, who didn't encourage upward mobility, because wanting "success" in life was akin to sinning. Whoever he was, with his hat over his face, he also didn't know I'd given all my energy to my boys, so they could fly and be free while I paved the road. Even then, God had taken one from me.

I've served my purpose. Now, leave me alone.

I stood and started to walk away, only when I whirled around, it was nighttime now, the stars in the sky burst like raindrops in a puddle, the ocean roared in my ears, the air was actually cold, and there was water pooled around my feet. I scrunched my toes in the sand to make sure I could feel them.

I was awake.

I'd sleepwalked?

Something cold and metallic touched my toe. I bent to lift it, the odd dream still vibrating in my chest, my hands shaking badly. Even in the moonless night, I could see it was some kind of bauble—round, silver, with a cutout swirl design. Obviously, a piece of someone's necklace, broken off as they'd tried to swim in the waves.

A chill wrapped around me. The ocean—dark, omnipotent, greedy—called to me. *Come home.*

"No way," I growled and headed back into the house.

· · ·

I'd never needed a café con leche as badly as I did the next morning, but ever since Pablito died, I hadn't drank a drop. My sweet boy had always made it for me with loads of milk, sugar, and a dusting of cinnamon on top. *Qué rico.* I would never drink it again. Instead, I'd switched to tea, and watching me make a mug at *House of Dolls*, then sit at the dining table to slowly enjoy it, one might've thought I was one of the guests now. But Lily did say I could have anything I wanted since the Montero House kitchen was about to be demolished.

Besides, I could not deny myself one of Lily's famous key lime croissants, featured on her show—at least, that was what Maya, the other housekeeper, told me. Over breakfast, I remembered my dream. Who was that man? And why had I not noticed walking in my sleep all the way out to the beach? At least I didn't have to deal with any seed-throwing monkeys this morning, although I did find an iguana on the front porch of this house when I arrived.

"Good morning," Nanette sang, checking her iPhone while her grandson, Sam, strolled in behind her, a bit like a puppy on a leash.

He gave me a chin tilt that said *'Sup*, chains from his pants jangling as he walked.

Lily Autumn was having a meeting this morning at 9 AM with the entire staff in the new community theater, the one Evan's team had just finished building. As people began arriving, I didn't want to appear like I was off the job, so I stood, tossed the rest of my tea, and followed the crowd through the living room, waiting at the double doors while others entered first. When it came to rank at hotels, house-keepers were the bottom of the totem pole, and although she'd said "everyone," I still had my doubts that they needed the cleaning staff for a big meeting.

I watched as the big players arrived—Katja in a fetching black jumpsuit, Lily in a turquoise and brown sundress, a gorgeous man wearing a captain's hat, two older ladies, one in a caftan, one wearing shorts and Birkenstocks, plus a whole bunch of people with tablets, clipboards, and electronic pens for taking notes.

"The production crew," someone said next to me.

I turned.

"Hiya." An older man in his sixties, channeling Jimmy Buffett in a baseball cap that read *Fish Want Me—Women Fear Me*, extended his hand. "I'm Sid."

"Regina." I shook his hand, took in his stonewashed jeans and Izod shirt, then shyly angled my body toward the wall. Sid was close, not inappropriately close, but close enough for me to see the sparkly specks in his blue eyes.

Luckily, surprisingly, he seemed to take hints well and put some space between us, continuing to greet everyone who walked by. Judging from the hearty hellos, I gathered he was not to be feared, and that the staff liked him well enough.

Lily walked onstage and tapped the microphone. "Welcome to *House of Dolls Theater*, everyone!"

A round of loud applause echoed through the auditorium. About twenty-five or so people had gathered. Lily made a gesture for anyone in the back to please close the doors, which I did, then took a seat in the last row. At the opposite end were the other new housekeeper, Maya, who was in her mid-to-late twenties, a new, beefy security guard, and other members of the cleaning staff. Then, there was me alone at this end. The odd man out.

I spent the next minute playing with the bauble I'd found in the sand last night, which I'd put on a simple chain and worn around my neck as a reminder that life was weird and sometimes you sleepwalked. The pretty little silver ball was about three-quarters of an inch in diameter with a brushed metal antique quality to it that I loved.

"Glad to see you all." Lily pushed glasses onto her nose and looked down at her notes. "First off, if you're here, it's because I value you. You're important to me, and you're important to this company. Thank you for being here. *Dead & Breakfast* wouldn't be what it is without you."

A smattering of applause followed.

Out of the corner of my eye, I caught sight of the woman I'd seen yesterday with the child on the stairs watching me. I knew nobody could see her because she was wearing a red-and-black dress like she'd hopped straight out of a cowboy saloon, feathers in her hair, and the bottom half of her body was missing. She strode to the front of the theater to listen to Lily.

"Let me just say, on the eve of Season two taping, that things are growing quickly," Lily said, leaning into the microphone. "The fans are here. They're stopping by as they drive through the Keys. They're waiting for me at the end of Key Lime Street. They're driving by the house and snapping pictures. They're taking photos of Jax at Publix."

Everyone laughed, and the guy wearing the captain's hat took off the cap and bowed.

Lily gave him an adorable look before going on. "We got the county to come out and place barricades at the end of each street, so that's good. When you drive up for work, show your ID to Serge, and we'll let you through. Serge, where are you?"

Serge, the security guard sitting with Maya, lifted his hand high and waved.

"We have the number one show on *The Cooking Network*, guys, so it's going to be a little crazy. Hang in there, keep an eye out for each other, all will be fine." She flipped a page in her notebook. "Next item on the list...I want you to meet new members of our team. Say hello to new kitchen and house-keeping staff, Ana Maria, Jaylin, Maya, and Regina."

Dozens of heads turned, as light applause filtered through the auditorium, and my stomach plummeted into my knees. I resisted the urge to sink into my chair. Members of a team? I couldn't recall ever getting a spotlight put on me this way—ever, in all my years of working. Housekeepers may as well have been invisible. Nobody looked at you when you were a maid; nobody expected anything from you either.

Resisting the urge to hide, I waved meekly. Thankfully, Lily went on with the meeting while my heart calmed down. I even managed a smile when the little girl from yesterday came twirling and dancing down the left side aisle toting a doll in her hands. She reached her mama who scooped her up and kissed her.

So, that was why this place was called *House of Dolls*, why dozens of beautiful figurines of every size and color wearing all matters of gorgeous chiffon and silk and satin dresses sat in cubicles around us with spotlights on them. And this theater... As I let my gaze wander, I saw them— men in suits and hats with thick mustaches who hadn't been there a moment ago sitting in the seats. *Ugh.* It was one thing to see a ghost or two, but not a whole room full of them.

I clutched the charm around my neck and closed my eyes, willing them to go away. *Close the eye, say goodbye. Close the eye, say goodbye.* When I reopened them, the men, along with the mama and child ghosts, were gone. I took a deep breath and slipped out the side door marked EXIT.

Maybe I shouldn't have taken this job. I should've known this would happen. I spent so long suppressing my "sight," but leave it to a walk on the beach to bring it back again. Once people found out, all anybody ever wanted was to talk to their dead relatives, and if I kept it a secret, all dead relatives ever wanted was to talk to their living loved ones. I'm sorry, but I was not an iPhone for the dead.

I needed grounding, so I opened the broom closet, picked up a Swiffer, and started cleaning ceiling fans, a very real job in this very real world. Ceiling fans were the number one neglected part of any house. Nobody wanted dust bunnies in their pain au chocolat, now, did they? Grounding, grounding...fancy furniture? Check. Gorgeous wraparound veranda? Check. Iguana watching you from that wingchair with one eye on you?

Uh...

"Hi. Regina, right?"

I whirled and nearly Swiffed off Katja Miller's face. "Oh, my goodness. I'm so sorry."

"No worries." She spit out a bit of dust and rubbed the spot on her cheek where my cleaning cloth had grazed her. "Didn't mean to come up behind you like that."

"There's an iguana." I pointed to an empty wingchair.

"Ah, you saw Callie." Katja smiled. "So, I'm not the only one."

"Callie's an iguana?" I asked.

"Callie's the spirit of a little girl who lives here," she said, waiting for me to react, but I simply stared at her. "Sometimes she manifests as an iguana. Assuming that was her and not some other iguana. We are in the tropics, after all."

"And monkeys," I said.

She tapped her chin. "Come to think of it, I *have* seen one over on Mango Road. We don't know where he came from. Possible that someone left him behind when they moved. Monkeys aren't welcome in most places outside the tropics. Anyway, happy to meet you."

"Yes, same! I saw you yesterday, but you were busy. Congrats on becoming the new host."

"Thanks!" Her green eyes, framed by that perfect eyeliner, sparkled. "I just wanted to say hello and tell you that you're going to be great."

"I am?"

"Yes. When I got here last year, I felt weird and out of place. I wasn't sure of anything. I could've used a friend telling me it was going to be okay. Which it was, eventually. Lily and everyone here is so amazing. Everyone's so welcoming."

"I noticed that. Wait, so you're the new host but you've been here a year already?"

"I wasn't always the host. Lily hired me to organize this house after she bought it. That's why I came to Skeleton Key all the way from the Midwest. Can you believe it?"

"That's a long flight. Your arms must've been tired."

She stared at me a second before bursting into a chuckle.

"See, this is what I mean. You're already killing it. Oo, I like this..." She leaned into me and tapped the bauble-charm around my neck. "Does it have any special meaning?"

The moment she entered my orbit, I could feel her energy —high, creative, uplifting, but underneath was a woman still basking in sadness that things hadn't worked out the way she'd planned. Worried about her girls. Worried about their father.

An image flashed through my mind. For just a second. A flash of yellow...fabric...colorful flowers...then it was gone.

"SpongeBob?" I blurted. "A blanket or...?"

Shock in her eyes told me I'd screwed up. Where on Earth had I gotten that from? Her mouth fell agape. *My* mouth fell agape. "I am so sorry," I said. "I don't know where that..."

Her gaze fell to my fingers twiddling the bauble hanging from my neck. "You can see things." Her attention was elsewhere—far, far away.

"I see things *sometimes*," I whispered, a tightness in my chest. "Again, I'm so sorry."

"It's fine. I have to go." And then, Katja Miller walked off leaving me there with my confusion. And my Swiffer. And my shame.

three

THIS WAS WHY, my whole life, I'd smothered it. Nobody liked a sixth sense. Nobody liked when I saw straight through their souls, and who could blame them? I wouldn't like it either if some random stranger could instantly see how, where, and on what cartoon-themed blanket my ex-husband had cheated on me.

I felt terrible for Katja. I hoped she'd gotten rid of that SpongeBob blanket, because objects soaked in negative energy made it more difficult for people to move on.

I had to find a way of turning off my sight like I had in the days when I lived with Daniel's parents, or I had to leave this place. It was the proximity to the area where I'd nearly drowned as a child that was causing it.

I spent the rest of my workday making sure the three guest rooms upstairs were sparkling clean, minding my own business, even from the other new staff members who'd clearly formed a bond before I arrived. At six o'clock, I walked back to Montero House, soaked in the neon-colored sunset sky streaked with clouds, and sighed.

Why was it I could see the ghosts of others but never my own? If there was any spirit I wished I could talk to, it would be my happy-go-lucky, sweet, loving son who'd been a joy to be around ever since he was a baby. Not that Andreas wasn't a joy—he was my son, and I loved him—but Andreas was more like his father—practical, stingy with affection, slightly selfish, whereas Pablito was a mama's boy in every sense of the word.

Pablito, are you up there? Can you see me?

Do you have any idea how much I miss you?

No answer.

When I arrived back at the house, the last of the construction trucks were leaving, and the house stood forlorn and lonely against the royal violet eastern sky. According to Lily, she'd purchased the home after Atlantis Cruise Line made a lucrative offer to the entire community in order to get them to sell their waterfront homes, but Lily held out, stopping the company in their tracks. When that deal fell through, some angry Skeleton Key residents sold their homes anyway, privately to private buyers—one of them was Lily, looking to expand her business.

It was why there was only one neighbor on Mango Road, lovely old Mrs. Patisse to the left of Montero House, whereas the other homes had gone empty, making Lily's new acquisition look all the more desolate and haunted. Of all the houses I'd seen on Skeleton Key, it was the stateliest with its Greek columns, symmetrical design, and wraparound porch. I hated to say it looked like a plantation home, which hinted at slavery, but it was built in the early 1920s and did have a classic, Southern exterior.

Heading up the flagstones, I paused when I saw someone walking away, cutting through the overgrown front yard of banana, umbrella, and mango trees. An older man wearing a baseball hat. The one I'd met in the theater?

"Hello," I called out. "Can I help you?"

Lily had said to be careful and lock my doors at night since the house was empty, and sometimes fans of the show liked to trespass. But when the interloper glanced over his shoulder, I was pretty sure it was the same man as the theater.

"Oh, hey!" He took off his baseball cap and waved it in the air. I hopped up the steps to the house and waited for him to come back around the side. "Hello, again."

"Sid, right?"

"Yep, sorry if I startled you. I was just leaving you a little something on the front porch railing there." He pointed.

I followed his line of sight to the spot and found something wrapped in paper. I lifted it, peeked inside. "A fish?"

"Yellowtail," Sid said. "I caught way more than I could sell early this morning. Thought you might like one."

"Thank you. That's so kind," I said. It really was a beautiful fish, and so fresh, too. "I'll make it for dinner. If the kitchen's still there, that is."

"And if it's not, I'll cook it for ya. There, I helped."

"Yes." I smiled. "I appreciate it."

Sid leaned against the mango tree. "I live down the beach, way down at the end, but you'll mostly see me sticking my nose in everybody's business from my boat." He laughed to himself. "Guess that's what I'm best at."

"Like a neighborhood watchdog, I take it?"

"Let's say watch-barracuda."

I chuckled quietly, stood there, unsure what to say. Was he waiting for an invitation in? Because I didn't know him from a hole in the wall, he was a bit too old for me, and I'd never invite a stranger into a house that wasn't mine anyway.

"I..."

"No, no. You don't owe me anything," Sid said, scratching his head through the baseball hat. "Not even conversation. I understand it makes women feel uncomfortable when a man presents them with a gift, like they owe them something. Not me, so no worries there. And you just getting home tired and all. I'mma make myself scarce now." He gave me a two-finger salute and started off again.

"We'll talk more some other day," I said, feeling bad. I didn't mean to come across as rude, but it was true that I was exhausted.

"You let me know if you need anything," he said, pausing when he reached the side gate. "Ms. Lily can't always take care of her people. She's a busy woman. That's why she's got me." He smiled a row of too-bright teeth against reddish skin, like someone had maybe gotten a dental whitening and a sunburn on the same day.

"I'm not used to the kindness," I blurted.

Sid paused, hanging onto the gate.

Where had *that* come from? Why was I being so honest with a man I barely knew?

He took a few steps back in my direction and stood with

his hat in his hands. "I understand that, Miss Regina. Is it Regina, or *Reh-hee-nah?*"

The way he pronounced my name the Spanish way, making an effort to honor my roots, probably because he'd noticed by my slight accent, melted my heart.

"Regina is fine," I said. "Or Reggie."

"Like Reggie Jackson." Sid mimicked a baseball player knocking out a home run, complete with cheering sounds and all. "Well, Reggie. I don't know about kindness. I haven't been kind to everyone in my day, but loyalty is another ball-game altogether. You're one of us now, so that means I'll be checking up on ya."

"You work for Lily?"

"I try to give her fish for free, Reg, but she insists on paying me, so yes. I suppose I'm a vendor. I provide all the *Dead & Breakfast's* piscatorial needs. Salty Sid, at your service." He bowed. "What brings you to Skeleton Key?"

"Besides a job?" I cringed.

He dipped his head. "That was dumb of me."

"You're fine. Only the job. I try to stay away from the Keys every chance I get."

He mimicked getting shot in the chest. "Ack, my heart. Them's fighting words, Reg. Who hurt you in these islands?"

"The Cuban government," I replied.

He took a moment to internalize then nodded. "Ah, yes. I understand that situation, being a native to these parts. So, coming to the Keys is like going home, in a way?"

"A bad way. Also, I'm not fond of water. Traumatic stuff when I was a kid. I'll tell you about it some other day. I'm going to go make dinner. *'So long and thanks for the fish,'*" I quoted and smiled.

He tilted his head, as a slow smile came to his face. "Douglas Adams. Great book, great book." Sid pursed his lips and whistled a tune, disappearing into the dense foliage that filled the space between Montero House and Mrs. Patisse's house.

Nice man, Salty Sid. Wholesome. Protective. I liked him immediately. I entered the house, fresh yellowtail on my mind, wondering how I was going to prepare it in this old kitchen without a functioning oven, when cigar smoke wafted into my nose, and old-timey music filled the air.

four

I WAS PRETTY sure I'd watched the last of the trucks leave as I came home, though the noises and smells said otherwise. Perhaps someone was still working or had left a radio on? A station played traditional, tinny, brassy sounds of a *son montuno*, the classic Cuban music typical of my grandparents' era.

I flicked on the first light inside the foyer.

"Hello?" I called out.

The odor of cigar smoke and tobacco leaf seeped into my nose, as I inched closer to the right side of the house where large flaps of clear plastic sheeting hung from ceiling beams like fluttering paper ghosts, separating the still-livable part of the house from the side getting a makeover.

Nobody replied.

The music got louder.

Against the back wall was an old fireplace. It was always funny for me to see fireplaces in Florida homes, since our weather was its own hellfire 360 days of the year. For Floridians, fireplaces were a luxury, but perhaps that was exactly why this classy dame of a home had one. It had once been a grand mansion by the sea. I reached out and ran my hand along the smooth marble mantel piece.

My veins turned chilly. As I slowly moved through the Montero House toward the side wing, my heart snagged in my throat when I caught glimpses of movement through the plastic. Were those people in there or reflections of dying sunlight in the dull plastic sheeting? The closer I approached, the more the reflections took the shape of figures, people milling about, some walking, but most seated at perfect intervals in rows. The music grew louder. I reached the plastic paint cloths and with shaky hands, separated two of them, taking stock of what my eyes were seeing—

A large room with high ceilings.

Men sitting at tables.

Busy hands.

Mounds of cigars.

Piles of them at numbered workstations.

I could only process it all in small chunks, because none of this had been here this morning, and I knew, without a doubt, that none of this was happening now. I was looking into a long-gone past. The music, the clothing, the architecture. Judging from the factory work shirts, the thick mustaches, and men's jackets and hats hanging on the wall, it was the 1920s or 30s, but that was impossible because behind me was evidence of a house being remodeled in current day.

The floor tiles were checkerboard black-and-white, the areca palms in each corner of the room lush green, and the sunlight streaming in through the tall windows bright, lemony yellow. So much color, more vibrant than any other visions I'd ever seen, more vibrant than even real life. I was used to random apparitions—an old lady here, a deceased family member there—but never an entire, vivid room like this.

A whole cigar factory?

I sucked in a deep breath after apparently holding one in. Could they see me? The workers rolled cigars diligently to the music, chatted in Cuban Spanish, and apparently couldn't tell that I was standing here in my jeans, polo, and sneakers ninety years into the future. Suddenly, the tunes scratched to a halt when a child operating a gramophone in the corner of the room lifted the needle, and a man, dressed in a nice suit and hat, newspaper tucked under his arms, cigar clenched in his teeth, entered to applause and fanfare. Confidently, he walked up to an elevated podium in the center of the room, announced what publication he'd be reading from today, and began projecting in a theatrical voice:

Béisbol en Cuba gana popularidad! His voice boomed. *Baseball in Cuba gains popularity.* He went on, reading from the newspaper of the day as the factory workers savored every word while their hands stayed busy. Every so often, the announcer would pause so the workers could discuss whatever he was reading and have good-natured debates.

It was in the middle of one debate about the best baseball teams when an Amazon of a woman strolled in, hands on hips, proudly parading the room. She watched each worker carefully, inspected the quality of their work, as they bowed their heads, restricted their talking, and sped up their pace. I half-expected them to catcall such a gorgeous goddess, but she was much too intimidating, mesmerizing to watch, with her beautiful flowing brown hair twisted over one shoulder, sun-kissed tanned skin, pants that accentuated her wide hips, thick heels, and a man's buttoned shirt ill-fitted to her womanly form. She was my age, matronly and compassionate in the way she tapped the shoulders of her workers, as if they—all eighteen of them—were like family to her.

But swimming underneath her watchful eye was a distinct sadness, and when she whipped her head in my direction, I tried to hide behind a column. But it was too late. Even as I held my breath, I could sense her shifting across the checkerboard floor diagonally, like a Queen toward me, a pawn in a game of chess.

I prayed she wouldn't see me, as she leaned back slowly, moving into my view. Our eyes connected. Her gaze roved down to my chest where I was nervously fiddling with my chain, then back up to my eyes.

Te veo allí escondida, she said in Spanish. *I see you there, hiding.*

"Uh-oh," I muttered.

Not again. Not direct communication with a spirit. It had been so long, and there'd been too many in one day. Better to get it over and done with.

"Can I help you with something?" I gasped all in one breath.

Looking at the workers first to make sure they were distracted enough and not engaged in whatever she was up to, she leaned against the column, locked eyes with me, and whispered, *Have you seen him?*

"Seen who?"

Ramón. He was supposed to be here two days ago but has not yet returned. She spoke in the quick, clipped dialect of my home island.

"Returned from where?" My voice was shaky.

She studied me a minute, dark brown eyes taking in my seriousness and sincerity. She did not want to say too much or clue me in on too much. That much was clear.

From his fishing trip, she said, lowering her gaze. *He was supposed to hire the new* lector de tabaquería *for us, but I had to do it myself.* She gestured toward the man reading from the center of the room. *At least they seem happy with him.*

I agreed the workers seemed happy with the lector reading aloud to them. "They do."

You haven't seen him? My husband?

"I'm sorry. I haven't." My blood felt cold. Too much spirit interaction made me sick. I backed away slowly toward the plastic sheet dividers.

Bastard. She clucked her tongue.

"I'll let you know if I do, though."

Sometimes, the promise for more was enough to make them let go of you. Sometimes they continued to hound until you gave them answers.

He said he would be back on Tuesday. It's now Friday...

"I'm sure he'll be back soon. You'll see."

I hurried off through the empty hallway toward the living room, glancing back once more to make sure the vision was gone. It was. All I could perceive now was a cold, dark empty room with freshly-fitted drywall, spackle, and dust all over the floor.

I didn't stop until I reached my room upstairs, locked the door, and hid inside the bathroom, waiting for the blood inside my body to run warm again. When it finally did, I realized what she'd been looking at so intently—the bauble hanging from my chain.

Thanks to disruptions in my sleep the last few months, I hadn't gotten any, so I read for thirty minutes, got out of bed, and began to dress. Pulling open a drawer in search of clean dark pants, I caught sight of Captain America. Sometimes, I kept on moving. Sometimes, I took out the T-shirt and held it to my nose, breathing in the lingering scent that used to belong to a bright, happy young man, then put it back.

Today, I held it up.

The whole left side of the red, white, and blue shield was covered in blood. Why did I keep it? Because it was all that I had. This and some handmade cards, letters, and drawings from his childhood days. His watch. His phone, which I'd gone through only once, just to look at his smiling selfies. Not much, honestly, which made me wish I'd been more obsessive about keeping things.

"You can visit me, you know," I whispered.

After a minute of waiting, hoping he'd reply, I rolled the T-shirt back up and put it away. Then, I hit the beach for an early walk to work. My last blood panel showed I needed Vitamin D, and where better to get it than straight from the sun?

Lily had asked us to enter the houses through the beach-side entrances over the next several weeks. Today was the first day of taping *Crone of Coconut Court*, and the front of the house would be set up for filming. Even from an eighth of a mile away, I could see the commotion up ahead. On the sand were lounge chairs taken by some of Lily's first guests to

House of Dolls. Behind them were a couple of production vans, their back doors open, booms, mics, and lighting equipment spilling out. It was only 7 AM, but already the sun was streaking rays of sunshine over a dark blue ocean.

Fifty feet away from the Gothic Victorian dollhouse was a covered cart and a man in khaki shorts and a blue T-shirt struggling underneath an attached umbrella. Judging from the illustration of a delicious ice cream cone melting on the side of the cart, he must've been a vendor, which puzzled me since I thought this whole stretch of beach was privately owned by Lily Autumn.

After some struggle, the man got his umbrella to stay open, and two younger women in pinup swimsuits sitting on lounge chairs applauded his efforts. He smiled at them and made a grand gesture of gallantly bowing to thank them. He turned around and saw me approaching.

"Morning!" He waved.

The lack of a boardwalk had me trudging through the sand. "Good morning," I replied, out of breath.

As an introvert, I had every intention of getting straight to work and starting my duties early with as little human contact as possible, but I was starting to see that minding my own business on Skeleton Key was going to be close to impossible.

The ice cream vendor was in his mid-to-late forties with a handsome face that paired well with the salt and pepper spray at his temples. Had he been wearing a suit, he could've starred as the sexy tycoon in any given soap opera back in the day.

The ice cream man reached out his hand just as I was passing him by. "Diego. Pleased to meet you." Up close, I noticed his closely trimmed beard and crinkly fine lines around bright amber eyes. His charming smile lingered an extra second too long.

"Regina. I work here," I said before he got the idea that I was a guest to butter up. I slipped my hand into his. He had nice, thick hands, the kind I could imagine choking up around a baseball bat, not selling scoops of ice cream.

What the heck?

I shook off my misplaced thought, but had trouble shaking Diego's smile as he tied a canvas sunshade to the frame of the cart. "Well, what do you know? I work here, too."

"You work at *Dead & Breakfast*?" I asked. "Shouldn't you be wearing a purple and green pinstripe butler outfit then?" I snorted.

He tapped his clefted chin. "Why didn't I think of that?" Either because he was honestly impressed, though more likely flirting with me, he pulled out his phone and jotted down the idea.

"Are you from around here?" I asked. "Or do you come a long way to sell ice cream?"

"Islamorada. Just a hop, skip, and a jump to the next island. What about you? Miami?" A question everyone from South Florida got, especially if you had a specific accent from any one of the dozens of Spanish-colonized countries south of here.

But how to answer where I was from? Cuba, originally. Then, Miami. Then, Pembroke Pines. Then, West Palm Beach. Now, as fate would have it, I'd dropped back down to where I'd started.

"The next house over," I decided.

"The Montero House?" He seemed genuinely impressed —or maybe it was concern—as he stacked paper cups next to sugar cones.

"Well, not really *from there*. Just staying there...for now. It's kind of lonely, not going to lie."

Whoa. Did I just tell a good-looking man without a ring on his finger, dimples, precocious eye crinkles, and a smile with enough power to light up the beach that I was lonely?

Diego beamed. "I see."

"What I mean is it's empty at night. After all the workers have gone home." *You're on a roll, Reg.* I dropped my head. "That sounds weird. What I'm saying is that...I have no idea what I'm saying. I'll see you around."

Tucking my shame under my chin, I walked away from Diego, who must've known how uncomfortable it made me feel to have him staring at me through his penetrating smile, as though I were simultaneously the most adorable thing in the world but also the most pathetic.

I had an excuse. I hadn't done this in a while.

"You know it used to be a cigar factory a long time ago, right?"

I slowed in my tracks. "I've heard. What else do you know about the place? It's a little...peculiar."

He opened a big silver cooler and stared into it. "If by peculiar, you mean haunted? You would be correct, Regina." His accent was half Puerto Rican, half Cuban.

"And? What else do you know?" I took a few hesitant steps toward him.

"I'm sorry, your thirty seconds are up. Please deposit another fifty cents if you wish to continue this conversation."

Diego set a tub of ice cream on the cart's counter and held out his hand to me.

I couldn't help but to smile-smirk. A widow like me had no business smiling so much. I slapped his hand playfully. "Cha-ching."

"Call continued. The first owner of the house, a Mrs. Vivian Montero, is said to haunt the place, along with a few factory workers."

"Hmm." I turned to go. "Tell me something I don't know. See you later, Diego."

"And she was one of the island's first witches."

five

I WHIRLED BACK AROUND. "WITCHES?"

Diego gave a slow, satisfied nod.

Did he mean the green-faced villains of cautionary tales for children? Mages who poisoned apples and set curses on the kingdom? Or more, *my* kind of witch?

When I was eight years old, a friend of the family had called me "brujita" during a party, all because I told her that her deceased great-uncle was standing behind her. My adopted mother sharply told them never to call me that again. I'd never thought of my spirit sensitivity as being a witchy characteristic. In our house, the word "witch" held a sinister connotation—someone in cahoots with the devil. But, to me, all it meant was someone with a natural ability to sense with their third eye, a skill anyone had or could cultivate if they wanted to.

"Well, if she was a witch, I'm sure she was a perfectly normal, nice witch," I said indignantly. I wanted to know more about Vivian Montero, the woman I was certain had looked deep in my eyes last night, but I had to get going.

"I'm sure of it, too. See you later, Regina." Diego smiled, slapped sunglasses over his eyes, then pushed his cart onto the beach, singing an old Cuban folk song that reminded me of days gone by.

That man—Lord have mercy.

Nice. Only problem was, he was an ice cream vendor, and I'd already been in one relationship with a penniless man. Any earnings Daniel and I ever made, we gave it to our home life, our kids. We never took breaks, never bought new things, never vacationed anywhere. The life of hustle was the life God had chosen for us, I'd been told over and over, and there was no shame in it.

Really? I always wanted to respond. *God wants us to serve and forever be...mediocre?*

"Good morning," someone said.

Captain Jax whisked by in a hurry.

"Good morning," I replied, still in a daze from my encounter with Diego. Nobody had the right to throw me off-kilter that way, but Diego had a lot going for him—looks, charm, humor...sinewy arms.

Inside the house, a hubbub was in progress. Lights, camera, action in every room. Last night, Lily had called to ask that Maya, the other girl, and I check every room in Berry House one last time before taping, then head over to *Sylvie & Lily's* on Key Lime Lane to spend the rest of the day. As I slipped into the stairwell, I brushed shoulders with Maya, who was coming down.

"A little late?"

I checked my phone. "It's 7:05." In her eyes, I saw understated ambition and perhaps the fear of never going anywhere.

"Like I said—a little late." She sashayed away in her tight black leggings and knotted up T-shirt. I was pretty sure we'd been asked to wear black pants, not leggings. If Lily Autumn had suddenly changed our dress code to allow bare midriffs, I must've missed the memo.

"*Alardosa*," I muttered under my breath. Why did younger women have to be so showy? Wasn't it enough that they were young and beautiful without showing off the contours of her ass?

At the top of the stairs, I paused when I saw the little ghost girl who lived here skittering and giggling from one room to another, ringlets flying out behind her. She poked her head out from the room to the left.

"I see you," I said.

More giggling.

Katja appeared from one of the bedrooms. "You see who?" She was breathless, fidgety, stroking her hair and fanning her carefully-crafted eyeliner. "Do I look okay?"

"You look fantastic," I said. "You're going to do great."

"I don't look like a middle-aged Goth prostitute?"

"What? Of course not. You look confident, stylish, totally in charge. Nothing like any prostitute I've ever seen."

She glanced at me.

"Not that I've ever seen any middle-aged Goth prostitutes. Believe it or not, you look marvelous." I wanted to add "for our age," but decided that wasn't necessary. She looked amazing—period. "I'm glad I ran into you. I wanted to say I'm really sorry."

She flipped her hair in a hallway mirror. "For what?"

"For what I said yesterday."

She paused and stared at me.

"When you came near me, I could sense something in you, and I said something inappropriate when I should've minded my own business."

"Oh, that? Pfft. Regina, right?"

I nodded.

She pulled out her lipstick and waved it around. "I was caught off-guard. I hadn't thought about *that*—what you said—in a while. Which is great. But. No need to apologize. You're not the only one with abilities here."

"I'm not?"

"Not to your degree of talent, but no. I'll have to introduce you to the ladies sometime. I'm sure they'll invite you to our next meeting in no time."

Next meeting?

"So, scaring people off with creepy abilities is normal around here?" I laughed.

From downstairs, a man called out Katja's name.

"Actually, it is. That's Kevin. I gotta go."

"Break a leg," I said and watched her fly off down the stairs. So, she wasn't mad? Who did she mean by "the ladies?"

For the next half hour, I moved from room to room with my rag and spray bottle, wiping down surfaces, even if they were already clean, just to give them that extra shine in case the cameras made their way up here. Everything was in order in these ornate rooms filled with moody, brooding, creepy dolls, and for once, I loved the place I'd been hired to clean.

I slipped downstairs past the production crew and out the back patio, glancing at Diego serving ice cream to a gay couple in matching black bathing shorts. Then, I was off to the other house. There were guests there, too, sitting on lounge chairs on the sand, but things were considerably quieter. No director Kevin yelling orders, no crew members hustling about at the last second, just the quiet bubbling of waves on the sand. Funny how water could evoke peace in one setting, but PTSD in another.

By the time I entered the house, I was already sweating from the long walk in the bright morning sun. I reached the back gate and pulled on the brass handle that led into the home's side garden—a tropical oasis. From what I'd been told, Lily and Jax had accidentally found a hidden distillery underneath this garden while working on a broken statue, and the whole place had received a well-deserved makeover. Me, I hadn't had a chance to see it for myself, so I took my time strolling through the lush, tropical, and green garden. Traveler's palms, key lime trees, birds of paradise, banana trees, fan palms, ferns, and monstera, all divided by a wandering cobblestone path. Butterflies flit about, as well as a few dragonflies. A beautiful place to meditate and call home.

Next to the garden was a small, brand-new modern building that served as a museum to the legacy of Annie Jackson, one of the island's first entrepreneurs, a woman who'd owned and operated a secret distillery during the days of Prohibition while selling key lime pies in her legal store-front. Beside the entrance was the famous mermaid statue I'd heard about, and it did, in fact, seem like the siren was staring right at me.

I hurried up the side steps and entered the house through the auxiliary door. These homes were so different than anywhere else I'd ever worked. Sure, they clearly had money put into them, but there was warmth and love and quirk and charm and coziness about them as well. No sterile grays and whites here. No gold accents and vast marble floors. The homes had been restored to evoke the Victorian days of yore in the Caribbean with their wide-paddled, slow-moving ceiling fans, tall windows to let in the bright light, and their potted palms.

Lily's house was quiet. Of course, it was, with everyone over at *House of Dolls*. A chef walked past me with a clutch of eggs in her apron, another with a chalkboard menu under his arm. Two housekeepers were busy brushing clean the dining linens, and Maya was in the corner, chatting up another one. Did that girl ever work?

I headed upstairs to take care of the guest rooms, as Lily had instructed. At the top landing, an enormous white cat was curled up watching the action all around, one green eye and one blue eye not missing a single beat. Also curled up next to him was the same gray kitty that had followed Lily into the Berry House the other day—a Russian blue with golden eyes. When she saw me, she extended a paw, yawned, and got up to stretch. Then, as I watched, she curled up again *inside* of the big, white cat's body, settling into the exact same position. The big white cat didn't seem to mind.

"I see you, ghost kitty," I said.

Alright, I was enjoying seeing ghosts again. They were people, after all—or cats, in this case—like anybody else, except they were dead and just didn't know it or didn't care. With Daniel gone, I didn't have to feel guilty talking to them. Ghosts weren't scary. It was Daniel's family that would continue to haunt me every day, but that was a whole other suitcase to unpack.

I got to work cleaning. So many beautiful things in each room. Crystals, tarot cards, glass spheres, paintings featuring celestial bodies—stars, the moon, the sun, comets, galaxies, nebulas, astrological symbols, constellations, and more. Each room was more beautiful than the next with more potted palms, ferns hanging in macrame hammocks, and a coffin-shaped shelf filled with more mystical things—geodes, figurines of gods and goddesses—all so different from the home I grew up in, yet very similar in its spirituality.

The very items my religion had taught me were not to be touched or looked at were similar to things they used—candles for prayer, oils for anointing, figurines of deities, saints, spirits, the Holy Spirit, the unholy ones, magic and religion, religion and magic. The lines were blurrier than they were drawn, and I understood them both. I walked the hedge, so why should I stand on one side of the theological fence?

I was entranced by these objects I'd been discouraged from learning about. What was so wrong with wanting to connect to a spiritual side, speak to the dead, to find out their secrets, to help them cross over, or help them solve myster-ies, bring peace to the anguished living? Wasn't peace what religion was all about? What could bring more solace to a person than knowing their loved ones on the other side had made it?

If I could know that Pablito was okay somewhere out there in another realm, that he hadn't suffered in the car accident, that he'd swiftly been launched into the ether then dreamily drifted into the cosmos in a cloud of calm and happiness, that would be such a gift to my broken heart.

Imagine how many other broken hearts could begin to heal with the simple gift of knowing!

My heart hurt to think about it. I quickly ducked into the adjoining bathroom and closed the door so I could have a private moment to cry. How was I supposed to live a full and happy life knowing one of my children was not in it? Daniel's departure had saddened me, too, of course, but it was different. Like me, Daniel had had a chance at life whereas Pablito had his whole life ahead of him. He'd been on his way to a party with friends Daniel didn't know, friends not from the church, friends he liked to talk about. Other friends. Daniel hadn't liked them.

They're sweet kids, I'd told him. Unlike Daniel, I'd met them.

They're irresponsible, Daniel had insisted.

But they hadn't been. I knew this for a fact. They'd just been in an accident the same way anybody else could've been, but Daniel used Pablito's new friends as leverage to show why straying from a path got you in trouble. Over the next few months, he started making me feel like our son's death had been my fault, like he might still be here if I hadn't encouraged his natural sense for exploration, if I hadn't urged him to go, get out of our rigid circle, experience all the things I hadn't been able to experience. Yes, I'd been his biggest cheerleader, so yes, part of me would always feel like his death was my fault.

I bawled.

I cried so hard, I went through what was left of the toilet paper. I sat there a long time, staring at the thick layer of white paint on the door. I cried until my contact lenses were fuzzy from the proteins in the tears, until I hiccupped out my pent-up pain. Then, because houses weren't going to clean themselves, I stood, washed my face in the sink, and nearly jumped out of my skin when I spotted a face behind me in the mirror.

"Geez!" I gripped the edge of the sink. "What do you want?"

The female face was older, kind, and concerned for me. She backed away and disappeared through the door.

"Sorry. I..." *Ugh.* I scared her away.

Trembling, I turned the knob and found the whole woman standing inside the guest room. Her hair was half blonde, half gray and wispy, and she wore a beachy tunic with flip-flops. Kind, smart, and sort of hippie-ish. She was pointing to the closet.

"You want me to open that?"

She nodded.

I would help her, whatever she wanted, but then, I had to ground myself and keep working. I couldn't spend every day being a ghost liaison. Slowly, I opened the closet with caution. Inside was empty, except for a few dresses hung by the guests. I was nervous. I did not want to be accused of searching through anyone's things, so I shook my head.

"No," I told the spirit. "I can get in trouble."

There. See it? she seemed to say, though I couldn't actually hear her. She was pointing to a little side hatch inside the closet near the floor with a latch over it.

I tried opening the latch. "It's locked."

Sometimes ghosts wanted to show you things that were no longer there during current day. They had no concept of time, so they had no way of knowing their belongings were gone. Except, as I watched, the ghost lady slowly faded, and a moment later, the latch began to move. It made a little creaking sound until the whole thing swung upwards.

Well, then.

On my knees, nervous that someone might find me, I scuttled forward and lifted the door. Inside was dark, humid, and drafty, but there was enough ambient light to see. Boards. Wooden, glazed, dark wood, light wood, dusty. Very dusty. I pulled one out and blew on it. Not just boards.

Spirit boards.

Communications boards.

Ouija boards.

Don't touch it, I could hear Daniel now: *Play with fire, and you'll get burned, Regina.*

"Quiet." I bit back guilt welling up inside of me.

Yep, they were Ouija boards alright. Nice ones, too, beautifully handcrafted in the old days. Lettered from A to Z with YES, NO, 0 to 10, and GOODBYE, these were the same type of boards I used once when I was little, when a neighbor who'd babysat me introduced me to one, before my grandmother found me out and made me get rid of it, except these were nicely crafted, not made by Hasbro.

In an instant, I knew the lady wanted me to take one. She'd seen me crying in the bathroom. She knew what I needed, and she had a solution. I also knew that her name had been Sylvie.

six

SNATCHING the honey-varnished board along with its heart-shaped planchette, I hid the items behind an armoire in the hallway until the end of my shift. I hadn't used one of these in forever, but maybe it was time to try again. It was possible I'd conjured up other spirits easily, because I *hadn't* wanted to talk to them. In my experience, wanting something badly made it stay out of reach.

By Sylvie's prompt, I'd try the method out tonight, and while at it, try helping Vivian locate her husband, Ramón, as well.

In the evening, I snuck the Ouija board under my shirt and headed out. Did I feel bad taking something from Lily's house without permission? Yes, but the house's previous owner told me to take it. That counted on some level, didn't it? I doubted anybody needed it right away, judging from how well-hidden it was, and I'd put it back when done using it.

When I crossed Coconut Court on my walk home, I noticed cars lined up behind the barricade on the far end of the street near the highway; fans clamoring to get a view of Lily, Katja, or any of the other residents who regularly appeared on the show. I waved to Serge, the security guard, stuffing a tissue up one nostril. I showed him my lanyard, and he waved.

When I reached my street, I turned left toward home, passing 70s style Keys houses, many of them empty because of how many residents had sold after the Atlantis Cruise fallout. The rest were undergoing some level of renovation. Seemed the whole island was getting a facelift. Must've been nice having money, not only to buy island homes but for makeovers.

I tried not to feel resentful. In my forty-seven years, I'd known rich people who were mean and rich people who were nice, poor people who were kind and poor people who were assholes. Money didn't make you a better or worse person—it took who you already were and elevated it. If you were already prone to kindness, a million dollars made you a kind millionaire. If you were prone to rudeness, a million dollars made you a rude millionaire.

When Daniel used to argue that money was the root of all evil, I'd remind him what I'd do with it if I had it—share. Did that make me evil? He always had some response that ignored my point. Daniel simply wanted to believe what had been ingrained in him from an early age, that we were better people simple, humble, and poor. After meeting Lily, however, I knew that was a crock of shit. One could be rich and kind as well.

Rolling down Mango Road was a van I'd seen earlier, and for the first time I noticed the name of Diego's ice cream business splashed across the side: *The Sweet Spot*.

My eyes popped open.

Is that so?

Look, I'd married early in life to a man who, God forgive me for saying this, never had a sexy bone in his body. If Daniel was sexy, it was because he was a good husband and father, a kind man who'd never hurt a fly, but he never made any efforts to understand my "sweet spot." The idea that a man might know where that spot might be was so foreign to me, I couldn't fathom it. I might've explored my sexuality more had I not tied myself to a relationship so early in life, but unfortunately, at my age, my chances were probably over. At least they felt that way.

Diego honked what sounded like a boat horn. I waved at the van slowly inching down the road. A tanned hand stuck out the window. "Headed home?" His gorgeous smile was so effortless, so natural, I knew he had to have women lined up at his door when he got home.

"Yes. Long day," I called, gripping the Ouija board under my shirt. I probably looked like I had indigestion.

Suddenly, the van stopped, and he hopped out. Uh, oh. Was he going to ask me what I was hiding? *Relax, Reg. He's just getting you ice cream*, I told myself the moment I saw him opening the back doors and yanking out his silver cooler. He scooped up a paddle of something orange and creamy.

"What's this?" I took his little wooden paddle offering.

"Mango ice cream."

"Yum!" I popped the paddle into my mouth. Sweet bébé Jesus, that was delicious—smooth, bold mango flavor, not too sugary, more about the fruit's natural sweetness. "This... is...amazing. I could eat a whole bowl."

Diego's sunny cheeks warmed. His voice dropped a notch. "Good, eh?"

If he could make other things the way he made ice cream, I'd be willing to overrule my "too old" theory. "Good? This is fan-freakin-tastic. You make this yourself?"

"Does it surprise you that I can?"

"I didn't mean it like that. I'm just shocked at how good it is."

"You think that's good, try this one." I'd pumped him up. Now he was reaching into a separate cooler in the back marked "coco" and scraping creamy white ice cream onto a mini waffle cone. "Here."

When he handed it to me, I noticed the way his chunky silver bracelet shone against his bronzed wrist. I tried the spoonful of ice cream—strong, sweet, tropical coconut—a flavor that would forever remind me of when I lived in Miami. "You have *got* to be kidding me."

"Girl, I have flavors here you've never tried."

My lips parted, as I stared at Diego showing off his chilled ice cream buckets like they were beautiful women in his harem. I had zero, zero doubt that he was right.

"I have mamey, mantecado, key limoncello, orange cream dream, piña colada, passionfruit..."

My tongue started sweating.

"Lychee, starfruit, papaya..."

My forehead broke into a fevered perspiration, and my lower extremities transmuted to gelatin. Besides being a fruit, papaya was a Spanish euphemism for lady parts, and Diego, hailing from Hispanic roots, *had* to know this.

"Mamoncillo, dulce de leche, café con leche..."

I died.

"Guarapo..."

I died again.

"Basically every tropical flavor you can imagine and then some. But my all-time favorite is mango. Have you ever eaten a slightly overripe mango?"

He blew out a puff of air.

I knew this was about to get good.

"Of course, you have, you're Latina. So, you know how good it is to pull the fruit apart, get all in there...it's juicy and dripping all over your face, but you don't care, right? Because you're in heaven, and when you're done, you have this happy, sticky mess. The absolute best. Anyway, here, take some for the road."

As Diego took a paper cup and scooped more mango ice cream into it, I went boneless. I hoped he kept a mop in the van for when women turned to puddles on the sidewalk. Those were a lot of high-octane words for a widow to hear.

The Ouija board fell out from under my shirt. "Oh, uh..."

"Need help?"

"I'm good." I took the cup of ice cream and squatted to pick up the spirit board I'd birthed on the sidewalk.

"*Bueno*, see you in a few days." He flashed his grin, tapped the double doors of his van, then hopped his hot ass back into the driver's seat and drove away.

I stood there trying to stitch words together. "Mmfango...snababa..."

A happy mess.

Juicy and dripping.

Hot ass?

What was happening to me? Who was I? A sad, lonely

woman who hadn't had sex in over two years and had never had good sex—that's who.

I pulled myself together, made it into the house and bathroom, where I sat in the tub under the shower and tried to wash away all thoughts of a man I'd only met this morning. Not because I was afraid of my feelings, but because I was afraid of my feelings. I'd just gotten out of one 30-year relationship with a man. Last thing I needed was another.

I'd never been with another man besides Daniel my whole life. I wouldn't even begin to know how to flirt, or act, or show interest in Diego, assuming he was even interested in me. But it was a moot issue, because I wasn't here to get distracted by an ice cream man.

If I was going to get distracted by anything, it was the board I'd taken—been given—from *Sylvie & Lily's* in order to try and contact my son. Assuming it even worked, what would I say? How sorry I was I couldn't protect him better? That I wished he wouldn't have gotten in that car or gone down that particular road? That I wished he would've stuck to the safe route and come to church with us, if only to keep him alive and with me a little longer?

As I'd done thousands of times since Pablito passed, I cried it out in the shower, letting my useless, tired tears go down the drain. *At least you had him for twenty-five years. At least you got to see him grow up.* It was true I was grateful, but I would never not want him on Earth again. I was selfish that way.

Stepping out of the hot shower into the cold air-conditioned room, something caught my eye. There, to the right, sitting on top of the Ouija board on the bed was a cluster of white and pink flowers. Five petals each. I picked one up and inhaled it. Sweet, strong, rosy. Plumeria, or frangipani as they were known around here.

I knew for a fact they hadn't been here when I first got home. I'd set the Ouija board on my bed, and now flowers were on top. Did someone come in while I showered? Who? Nervously, I changed into shorts and T-shirt, grabbed a 2x4 section of wood I'd stolen from the construction site as a weapon to keep in my room, then opened the bedroom door slowly.

If I saw Vivian and her cigar rollers again, I'd be okay with that. Ghosts weren't a problem. It was real, live people I feared. From downstairs, I heard a soft rattling in the kitchen. I choked up on the 2x4 like I was up to bat, then slowly crept downstairs. The sounds of something cardboard-like falling to the floor reached my ears, followed by a chirping noise.

Maybe this was a bad idea, staying at this house. Maybe I wasn't ready to be alone surrounded by ambient noises, most of which were alien to me. Maybe I was tired of living in fear and wanted to press an imaginary "reset" button on life.

"Hello?" I called.

Another chirp flitted through the foyer, and that was when I saw the shadow creature on the wall—enormous, lumbering, hunched over, clawed hands around a paper cup...sinister! I turned the corner.

Small. Harmless. Monkey.

I put the 2x4 down. "You." I caught my breath.

The capuchin, whose face was covered in melted mango ice cream, swiveled on his butt to face me, then handed me the empty cup. *More?* he asked with the tilt of his face.

"We're fresh out, buddy."

He pressed one hand to his mouth as he scratched his head with the other while absorbing my response. Suddenly, he skittered off to God knows where and as I sat on the bottom step thanking the universe for not making today the day I died at the hands of a flower-gifting serial killer, the monkey came back with an underripe coconut.

"Where did you get that?"

He handed the green ball to me.

"Anywhere. You got it from anywhere. This is the Keys." I took it and pretended it was too hard for me to bite through. "It's not ready. See?"

Then, I swear on my life that the following happened—the capuchin picked up the empty paper cup, held it in one hand, and pointed at his wide-open mouth with the other.

I snorted. "Wait. You want me to take this coconut and make more ice cream with it? You think I made that mango ice cream out of the mango you gave me? You're cuckoo *en la cabeza*, you know that?"

The monkey looked seriously insulted. He took the paper cup, cocked his arm back, and launched the empty ice cream cup at me, conking me in the head.

"Hey!"

He disappeared through the wide-open living room littered with drop cloths, planks of wood, and stacked tiles into the even larger, emptier space where I'd seen a working cigar factory just yesterday. At least he hadn't thrown the coconut at my head.

I stood in the empty room, resting my hand on the fireplace, as I roved my gaze over the construction, loving the way the smooth, lovely marble felt under my fingertips, imagining Vivian and her family living here long ago. I hoped the workers would leave this room alone, the fireplace intact, preserve some of the house's vintage integrity.

But who was I to have an opinion? Never would I ever own a house like this anyway, not with what I earned. Even with the decent pay I was getting, the most I could ever hope for was to rent a comfortable apartment near Andreas one day when the time came. I shouldn't even stand here imagining it. Dreaming came with a hefty price tag of disappointment.

I left the room and went upstairs.

seven

NEARLY A WEEK of working and cleaning, cleaning and working. As much as I wanted to engage in a personal séance with Sylvie's board, work at *Dead & Breakfast* kept me busy. Even my encounters with Diego were measured in seconds, mostly because I couldn't afford that kind of distraction. I awoke each day remembering why I was there —to do a job, stay focused, and make a buck or two.

During one of my breaks, I sat on a piece of driftwood on the beach between *House of Dolls* and Montero House, away from the bed-and-breakfasts, reading. Lily never asked me to stay away or be "invisible" like other employers had, but I'd done it enough times now to know it was what guests wanted. Nobody liked to see older women in domestic housekeeping roles on their breaks. It made them feel sad and helpless, similar to seeing a homeless person sitting on the side of the road. Nobody liked to feel uncomfortable about their own privilege, especially when they were on vacation.

I was eating pineapple chunks from a plastic container,

doing my best to avoid Diego who'd occasionally wave to me from down the beach, when I heard a bell mixing in with the sounds of seagulls fighting over the chance to eat my lunch. Within a minute, I saw the man again. Salty Sid, in his natural habitat—a small boat on the seashore.

He waved.

I waved back.

There was something wholesome about this man that made me totally not mind his interruption. He dropped a small anchor tied to a rope and hopped out. Like Diego had, he, too, rummaged through his cooler for something to give me. What was it about the men on this island and their coolers?

I watched him walk my way with another fish in his hands. A much bigger one than before. "How goes it?"

"It goes." I put down my book and looked into my pineapple container. "The other fish was great. Thank you so much." I hadn't cooked it yet, more like saved it in the freezer for when I had more energy.

"Here's another. Dolphinfish. Just a little one."

"That's little?" I gawked at the two-foot-long fish.

"For a dolphinfish, it is."

"You don't have to do this, but I appreciate it." I really did. This fish would last several days once I finally decided to cook it, relieving me from having to buy too many groceries. Plus, it was as fresh as fresh could get. I should actually throw it in a pan this time.

"It's no skin off my back, Reggie. How are you doing?"

"Ah, you know...cleaning. Then, more cleaning."

He rested his old, scuffed sneaker on the twist of drift-wood and stared down the beach, blue eyes catching the midday light just right. "It's a tough job, to be sure, this job of yours. I wouldn't know, but I respect it."

"I beg your pardon?"

"Housekeeping, a maid, cleaning service, whatever it's called these days. I can never keep up with the vernacular. It's considered by most people to be women's work, not skilled labor. Dirty and stigmatized as personal servitude." He shook his head.

"Yeah, actually." As much as it hurt to hear, it was nice that someone addressed it straight on, for once.

"Nobody likes to feel subservient or undervalued."

"You can say that again."

"You don't see many men doing it. Want to know why that is?"

"Because they're spoiled."

"That's right. From the start, boys see their mothers and grandmothers in the position of cleaning house, so for them it's normal to see women in these roles when really, all they're learning from a very young age is the normalization of the exploitation of women."

That wasn't what I said, but damn, Sid. Straight through my heart.

"It's not right, and it needs to change."

"I don't think it'll ever change, Sid. Unfortunately, it's a job and somebody has to do it."

"Fair enough, but the way employees are treated can change, and this is why..." He squatted on the sand, readying himself to teach me what I already knew about my not-so-chosen career.

I could smell his sweaty, fishy old man skin, and to be honest, I was not offended in the least.

"And this is why," he repeated, "it's important to have more women in higher positions of business and management. See here, you have Lily Autumn in charge of this place."

"And she's awesome," I said.

"She is. Why? Because she's respectful, because she values people, other women," Sid said.

"She doesn't make me feel cheap or dirty."

"Because you are not," Sid said sharply, as if he were my dad reminding me of my value. I never had a dad like that. "You are not, and Lily recognizes this. Why? Because Lily Autumn is an empathetic human being. You know what's the first class most boys should take in high school?"

"Bathing."

"Empathy," he spat.

I loved having women's issues mansplained to me, but I didn't mind it either, because Salty Sid was on the right side of the fight, even if he was a little clueless in his execution.

"Did you know..." Sid finally stood straight and arched his back, "...that women make up half of all employees in the hotel and restaurant industry, but because of gender stereotyping and discrimination, most of them will never see a managerial position, and if they do, they'll be paid less than their male counterparts?"

"Yes."

But what did he want me to do about it?

He must've realized he was bringing me down, because he said, "Bah. Now, I'm just blathering on." He waved his hand around. "Sorry, I tend to get on my soapboxes."

"No, it's a nice soapbox. I appreciate the sentiment. I just..." I didn't like addressing this myself, though it was a very important topic. I looked at him. "I don't know how I'm supposed to get out of this. I've been doing it all my life. I have no other marketable skills, and I don't have the time nor money to learn. I'm stuck, Sid."

He pressed his lips together in sympathy, hands on his hips. "You gotta show your talents. That's all. You've gotta have a secret skill hidden in there somewhere that you don't realize is a talent. Something you've always taken for granted. Something you can market. Think outside the box." He tapped his forehead.

"My box is tired, Sid." Scaring people with my ability to see through their souls was my only other skill. No, thanks.

"Gah, there's gotta be some way."

"I could teach housekeeping skills to other women," I said, "get in a managerial position that way, but that would be too much like passing the torch." I sighed. I felt myself on the brink of tears. "I'm glad I don't have girls. I wouldn't have made a very good girl mom."

I supposed I wasn't a very good boy mom either. All my boys ever saw was me do was bust my exhausted butt for a dollar.

"Don't say that, Reg. Any daughter of yours would be proud of their hardworking, intelligent mother. You hear me?"

I dipped my head. I gave him a sad, appreciative smile. "Thank you. I do have to get back now."

Felt like I was always saying that to someone. When did I ever get to relax a second and take time for *me?*

"Same here. Got a ton of lobster to drop off at Lily's. Want one?"

"No, thanks. I've got enough here for a week." I lifted the

dolphinfish an inch off my lap. "Thanks for taking the time to talk to me and not make me feel like I'm invisible."

Sid smiled but he wasn't satisfied with the outcome of our conversation and went on. "A smart woman in her prime, beautiful inside and out, is never invisible, Reg. Now, go knock it out of the park. And think about what I said, eh?" He shot an invisible dart at me from his fingertip then trudged down the sand. "I'll see you tomorrow."

"See you tomorrow."

I was so mesmerized by Sid walking away that I never noticed Diego flouncing up the sand. "Hey, my friend!" he said to Sid.

"Hey, yourself, kid. Do me a favor and get this girl some ice cream, will ya?"

"Already on it, boss. I was just coming to ask what flavor she was pining for today." Diego turned his bright, dimpled smile on me.

"Good man!" Sid raised both fists in triumph, as if ice cream could solve all my problems. At least it was a start.

Diego-flavored ice cream.

That's the ice cream I want today.

"I'm okay for now," I said instead. "Thank you. I really do have to get back to work." Though I truly loved how sweet and protective the men were here: like a pack of wolves, except less furry.

"You sure? Free homemade ice cream? All you have to say is which flavor, and it will magically appear."

Magically appear.

I thought of my little capuchin monkey, the way he threw fruit at me and expected it to turn into ice cream. Was life really that simple? You just asked the universe for a favor, and a favor it would provide? If that were true, why had I lost my son? Why couldn't I snap my fingers and find my bank account full of money? Why couldn't I turn back the sands of time and relive my youth in a different direction?

I had to rethink it all. For now, I had bedsheets to change.

"This call will soon end. Please deposit $0.25 to continue—"

"Coconut," I told Diego and tried something new and different—a smile. A slightly flirty smile. Why not?

I had the power to make him grin in return, to make him say, "Well, alright, alright," like a Latino Matthew McConaughey. "You want it now, or bring it by later?"

Oh.

Was he asking to come into Montero House or simply stop at my door? God, I was so bad at this. Did it matter? I had no one else to talk to. What was so bad about a cute guy stopping by to chat, especially if he brought me ice cream?

"Bring it by later," I said quickly before I could change my mind. He smiled. Small victory.

eight

MONDAY WAS MY DAY OFF, so of course I spent it doing totally relaxing things like going to the bank to deposit my check and buying groceries at Publix. In front of me in line to pay was a lady and her three blond children buying swim noodles, snacks for their beach outing (judging from the swimsuits, SPF lotion, and baby wipes). Me, I lived on the beach for free and hadn't had any time to enjoy it.

I had to correct this.

I would use the Ouija board. Tonight. There'd be a near new moon out, so I could sit on the sand under the cover of darkness but also have enough light to see the letters in case a ghostly visitor decided to spell out a message. That wasn't how most people enjoyed the beach, but I wasn't most people.

I should get candles.

Dipping out of line, I headed to the housewares aisle and found the candles on the bottom shelf. I squatted, looking for the tealights with my hand basket next to me. Behind me, a young woman wandered near, talking to her friend on speakerphone.

"Bro, because..." The young woman said. "That's how the current lady was hired."

"Because she was a maid?" the voice on the speakerphone asked.

"Not a maid, but a hired assistant at the house right after Lily Autumn bought it. After a few months of working there, my boss ended up hiring her to be the host."

I glanced over my shoulder. I was almost 100% certain it was Maya facing the opposite shelves, checking out batteries, with her long, brown hair pulled back into a ponytail. She also had the day off today.

"So, you're thinking that if you work there, too, you'll get hired for the next show?" The girl on speakerphone sounded amused.

"Bro, I don't even know if there *is* a next show, but it can't hurt to be in the right place at the right time, you know? This is the craziest shit I've ever done for an audition."

"But you don't even know if there will be one."

"Hey, you gotta take opportunities as they come. At the very least, I'm cleaning. My mom would be so proud. Where are the double A batteries? I swear they're always out."

"Someone in the Keys is having fun," her friend said.

They both laughed.

"Did I tell you what the ghost crew said..."

I snuck out of the aisle before Maya could see I was behind her, eavesdropping on her conversation, and hurried to the Express Lane, praying I wouldn't run into her again.

So many thoughts slapped the back of my head. Maya was only working at *Dead & Breakfast* as an audition in *case*

Lily decided to produce a third show? She was hoping to get noticed, so that Lily might hire her as the next host. So, she wasn't really a housekeeper? What a slap in the face to real housekeepers who actually needed work! And what was this "ghost crew" she mentioned?

Ack. It was none of my business.

Not that it surprised me, but I always felt Maya was too beautiful to be a housekeeper, although the faultiness of that idea raised more questions than answered them. Did that mean I might have a better job if I were younger and more beautiful? Was Maya right and Lily Autumn was scouting us for the next manager and host? Was I destined to be stuck in my job forever?

I paid for my items and scuttled out faster than a barefoot beachgoer being chased down by a land shark.

On my walk back, I couldn't shut up my brain. I thought I was here simply to work and mind my own business. I really hoped that was the case and not that Lily was hoping to discover a star in one of us. If so, she could gladly give Maya her big break, because I did not, under any circumstances, want to be on TV. That was one thing I was not cut out for.

However, it did rub me the wrong way that Maya was here under false pretenses. She was making a mockery of housekeeping, as if housekeeping weren't already a mockery of itself. Was this something I should bring up to Lily or keep to myself? After all, I wasn't supposed to hear that conversation, and besides, I didn't want to look like a snitch.

For all I knew, Lily might be thrilled to have employed a housekeeper who also happened to look the part, have acting experience, and bring great success to the show. After all, Maya did say this was the most she'd ever done for an audition, implying she was working towards a goal. No, it wasn't my business. I would definitely stay out of it. Stay focused, do my job, get paid, go home.

My phone rang, and to my surprise, it was Andreas, my eldest. "Hey, Mami."

"Hello, my love. What are you up to?" Andreas wasn't the type to call just to see how I was doing. Even at twenty-eight, he still called only when he needed or wanted something.

"Just here with Mel. We're looking at Expedia packages." In the background, Melinda gave me a weak hello.

"Oh? Going somewhere?" I asked.

"Hoping to get the heck out of Dodge and go to Paris. Maybe London. Rome or something."

"How nice," I said, waiting to see how I factored into this equation. Would he ask me how things were going at my new job?

"You've never been, right?" he asked.

I sighed. "No. I've never been outside of Florida. Papi and I never got the chance. I thought you knew that."

"That's what I thought," Andreas said. Then, it occurred to me—was he thinking of inviting me? Would I finally get the chance to travel to any city outside my home state? "So, I wanted to ask you..."

Here it was...

"Do you still have Papi's watch? The one he got from Tío Bob?"

His words confused me. "The Rolex he never wore?"

"Yeah, the nice one with the platinum band and the gold trim."

"Why?"

"Do you need it? Are you going to sell it?" Andreas asked.

"I haven't had the chance to think about it, Andy. Why?"
I knew now why, and my hopes deflated.

"Would it be okay if I sold it? It would help pay for this
trip, and the last place Melinda and I've had a chance to go to
was New York City, and that was four years ago."

"At least you had the chance to go." I sounded bitter but
did my best to change my tone, not let it affect me that my
son only called to ask me for his father's watch. "I'll see, but
right now, I'm in the Keys. I won't have a chance to get to
storage for a few months."

"Okay. Well, what about Pablo's stuff? Can I get in to see
some of his things? It's been three years, Mom. I think it's
okay if I go through his belongings. He would've wanted—"

"You know what? I'm about to cross a major highway,
and I need to pay attention. Why don't I call you back when I
get home?"

Silence on the other end. Sure, it was clear I was avoiding
the matter, and he was right, it was time to get rid of some of
Pablito's things. Yes, my son probably wouldn't have minded
that his brother hocked some of his items, but did we have to
talk about it now? Couldn't we go over it in person, together,
when I had the time?

"Sure, but don't forget," Andreas said. "We want to try
and book this tonight."

"I understand. I'll call you later. I love you, mi amor." I
hung up before he could hear the sting of tears in my voice.
Here I was busting my butt working a job I hated, without an
apartment to call my own, exhausted and feeling overemo-
tional, but he needed my help planning a trip to Europe?

I should've been thrilled he and my daughter-in-law
wanted to see the world. I should've felt a maternal satisfac-

tion at the chance to finance a dream come true for him. I should've been proud that my surviving child held a secure career as a math teacher and was able to travel, but I couldn't bring myself to feel the way he wanted me to.

What about me?

Did anyone care about my situation?

Did I matter to anyone anymore?

I felt like that poor tree in that Shel Silverstein book I read to my boys when they were little, giving and giving and giving of myself until there was nothing left and no thanks in return—used.

As it turned out, the night was blustery and rainy, so instead of the beach, I sat on the floor in one of the empty upstairs rooms, opened the windows to let in the March breezes, and surrounded myself with the lit candles. I placed Sylvie's spirit board in front of me, imagining a conversation with Diego, or Sid, or Lily going something like this:

So, what did you do on your night off?

Used a Ouija board to try and contact my son.

blank stares

I could've spent this evening any which way—reading, going for a walk, getting to know my neighbors or coworkers more, especially that Mrs. Patisse who liked to collect the fallen mangos off the ground. But no—dangerously dabbling with the occult sounded like a plan to me!

I was going crazy. No sane Catholic would ever do this. No sane non-Catholic either. I'd heard it all my life—play with a Ouija board and you end up inviting in unwanted entities. Thing was, I'd used it in secret as a child and it helped me hear the ghosts better. The most important part was praying for protection and saying goodbye if things got too intense, which they never did. I would be fine. As a mother who'd buried one child, I'd already been through enough hell. Nothing could hurt me anymore.

Letting out a sigh, I sat cross-legged and closed my eyes, hands on my knees. "Lord, it feels weird to be doing this again, but I ask that you protect me from unwanted energies. Allow in only the good, those who wish to communicate with me and those with whom I wish to communicate. Specifically, Pablito."

Then, for added benefit, I threw in a Hail Mary. "...Holy Mary, mother of God, pray for us sinners now and at the hour of our death. Amen."

Okay, that should be enough.

I lowered my shaky fingers to the wooden planchette. It was a nice one, hand-carved and varnished with a clear glass window instead of scratchy plastic. My fingertips touched the wood and I waited, imagining myself surrounded by God's loving light and Jesus's protective glory—a golden, luminous aura surrounding me.

The soft lapping of waves outside the window lulled me into a relaxed state, but I didn't go into any transcendental dimensions. I was just here, in the present, listening to the sounds around me, feeling the cool breeze, feeling alone but not disliking it. All my life, I'd spent it with Daniel and our family. Over the last six months, I'd learned to spend time by myself, and while I thought I would hate it, I had to admit I liked it.

For the first time ever, I could hear my own thoughts.

The planchette began to move. Slowly, softly. I knew it

was my own kinetic energy flowing through my fingertips, my own deep breathing moving it side to side, a few millimeters at a time. I went with it, thought of it as an extension of my own hand, and once it got into its own rhythm, I imagined Sylvie here with me guiding me along. The previous owner of Lily's home had been a family member of Lily's, that much I could tell, a loving spirit who accompanied her as much as a guiding light.

"Be with me, Sylvie," I said, because this had been her idea to begin with, and she was a strong presence, one who would never allow anything dark or evil to come through.

Within moments, I heard soft, warm breathing that might have been my own or could've been hers or another feminine presence, but it definitely wasn't my son's. I would've recognized him a million miles away.

"Is somebody here with me?" I asked, my own voice strong and clear in the silence of the house. "Is there a lady here?"

The planchette swayed back and forth between the D and the J, back and forth, a waiting signal.

"I know Vivian is here, in this house, as well as someone who left me flowers. Thank you, whoever that was."

The planchette's path widened and tilted so that it moved from an upper corner to a lower corner on the opposite side then up on the same side then opposite lower corner—a figure eight. I didn't need this board. After all, I could see the wandering spirits of this realm, usually when I least expected it, but something about the spirit board made it more concrete. Using it gave me the choice to speak to them, not the other way around, and I felt Sylvie was right—maybe this would help me reach Pablito.

After a while, the figure eight widened and sped up. My body tilted left and right to keep up with it. My eyes closed, so I wouldn't be tempted to spell out my own thoughts. "If you're here, I would like to know your name," I said. "As long as you mean me no harm."

Naming an entity gave it power, and I did not want any dark energies giving me their names here tonight.

The planchette dove to the bottom left suddenly. I opened my eyes. The window hovered over the N. "N," I said aloud. It swerved to the right a bit then returned, hovering over the O. Then, it moved over to the R, did another swoop to the right before sliding all the way across to the left and landing on the A.

"Nora?" The planchette settled back into its figure eight pattern. "Thank you for telling me your name, Nora. Are you the one who left me flowers?"

I felt that Nora was the one who'd left the plumeria. She was feminine, young, and playful. But she'd died tragically, and I didn't need to ask her to know it. Just to confirm. "Nora, did you die in this house?"

The planchette swiftly moved to YES.

"Thank you. Were you a young woman? Under the age of twenty?"

The planchette again moved to YES.

"Did you work here in the cigar factory?"

The planchette swiveled to the other side of the board—NO.

Hmm. I could sit here all night talking to Nora, but she wasn't the reason I was doing this. I didn't want to be rude and ask for my son, so I decided I would give her a chance to be heard. "Nora, do you want to tell me how you passed away? It's okay if you don't."

The planchette continued on its figure eight path for a few moments, then another, and after a minute, I thought maybe Nora had moved on or didn't want to talk about it. The soft scent of flowers filtered into my nostrils and when I closed my eyes again, I could almost see her—long, brown hair, flowing white dress that scraped the ground, hands clasped together.

She looked and felt like a younger version of Vivian. "Were you related to Vivian Montero?" I asked.

Without opening my eyes, I felt the planchette veer to YES. Ah, so something did happen. Vivian had been right to be anxious when I spoke to her. Right away, I felt a connection to the woman—she'd lost a child. Tears rose to my eyes, not only out of sympathy, but because again, I'd made contact with someone else's baby, not my own.

Tears dripped down my cheeks, but I didn't move my hands from the planchette. "Nora," I hesitated. "Is anyone else here with you? Is...there a young man, by any chance?"

The planchette remained on its figure eight path. Seemed that as much as I desperately wanted it to say YES, it wasn't meant to be. Maybe Pablito wasn't earthbound anymore. Maybe he was in Heaven, and I wouldn't see him again until I got there. I knew, in my heart, that I needed to accept it, yet I couldn't.

"Anything else you wish to tell me?"

I waited. The easy breeze blew a little harder, the bauble around my neck was swept aside, and the candles flickered. Suddenly, I heard, from very far away, the sound of men's shouts coming closer. In my mind's eye, I saw lanterns bobbing in the night along the beach, orange glow growing brighter, and saw Nora's flowing dress flailing out behind her as she tried to hide.

They were coming.

For her and her mother...

...and a baby, a little brother, sleeping peacefully in his bassinet while her mother worked a late night in the factory. Nora picked up and hid the baby in the closet, locked it, then closed the bedroom door. This same bedroom I was in right now. As the voices grew louder, my heart pounded as if they were coming for me.

Come out, bitches! A man shouted from the beach below, and a pounding came at the door.

nine

I SCREAMED, as my hands broke contact with the planchette. Placing my fingers on it again, I swiped across GOODBYE at the top. "Goodbye, goodbye," I muttered several times, just to be sure. My stomach heaved. I sucked in a deep breath to prevent full-on sickness.

Out of the corner of my eye, I noticed my phone screen lighting up on silent. I leaned over to see a text from my boss. "Hi! You home?" Again, I heard a knock on the door, only it didn't sound as loud as it had a moment ago.

Shit, Lily.

I could barely breathe.

Nervously, I typed back: *Be right there,* then took a moment to calm down. The shouts of angry men, the intensity, the desperation I'd felt coming from Nora...I shed each one like winter layers in stifling heat. Pacing the room, I focused on breathing deeply.

"You're fine, it's fine...it happened a long time ago," I said. Once ready, I blew out the candles and headed downstairs to get the front door. "Hey! Sorry, was in the bathroom."

Lily leaned up against the railing with Katja beside her, both smiling. Without her cat-wing eyeliner, shorts and T-shirt with messy hair, Katja looked like any random middle-aged lady. Like me. I liked her even more. "That's okay," Lily said. "I should've called first, but we were getting in our step count around the neighborhood and decided to come and check on ya. Can we come in?"

"Of course." I opened the door wider. "It's your house."

Lily glanced around at the progress the renovation crew was making. "Nice. I see they started work on the great room."

I looked in the direction she was pointing. "The cigar factory?"

"Is that where it used to be?" Lily's eyes lit up. "We were wondering that. There are no photos of the interior of the house from those days. I've searched everywhere. How did you..."

Katja gave Lily a knowing nod.

"They're definitely doing a lot," I tried saying something less incriminating. "It's fun to go to work each day then come back to see a new wall or floor put in."

Katja felt the smoothness of the new walls. "Agree. When they were working on *House of Dolls* while I was living there, I got to hear all the noise. After a while, it became a comforting sound."

"Also, because you met Evan there," Lily turned a smile on her. "The sound of construction means a lot more than comfort to you." She winked.

"True, true. Worth it." Katja smiled.

Lily smiled.

They both stood there, smiling. Their brains were definitely in different emotional spaces than mine. Why were they here? Did Lily find out I took the Ouija board, or did Maya tattle on me and tell Lily I was a few minutes late the other day, or maybe... I was so used to backstabbing in my line of work.

"I told Lily about the other day," Katja blurted. She wrung her hands and wore a guilty expression on her face.

I chewed the edge of a cuticle.

"When you told me about the SpongeBob blanket?"

"Oh." I covered my face with my hands. "I am so sorry about that. It won't happen again. You can be sure of that." I may as well march upstairs and start packing. It was nice while it lasted.

"We want it to happen again," Katja said.

"Excuse me?"

I was not about to be destroyed?

Lily brushed my arm with her fingertips. "My goodness, Regina, you're shaking. Come, let's sit out front. I think that's the only place to sit anyway. Are you comfortable here, or should we give you a room next door? I just thought since this house was bigger, that you might be more comfortable."

"Oh, I'm fine here. Totally fine."

"Are you sure? Not too haunted?" She laughed.

I said nothing, the ghosts too fresh on my mind.

They led me outside to the front veranda, a very nice front veranda that I hadn't had a chance to spend any time in, except for the day the little *mono* brought me a mango.

"I know it must sound weird to hear us say that." Lily sat on a rusty porch swing while I took a wooden bench opposite her. "But you must know that we don't mind people with special abilities like yours. If anything, we're intrigued."

Katja leaned against the railing. "Your gift does go with the *Dead & Breakfast* brand."

"I gathered that from the whole Goth vibe, but I thought..." How to put this...?

"That it was all for appearances?" Lily guessed. "Nah, we actually walk the walk and talk the talk here. We're witchy AF through and through."

"Which is why we're here," Katja added.

"We don't do this with just anyone, but we were wondering if you'd like to come to one of our hangouts. It's fun. You'll get to meet Heloise and Jeanine."

"And Sam," Katja said. "So talented."

"Maybe Thursday? Or whenever is easier for you." Lily looked at Katja for backup, and they both seemed to agree that Thursday was good.

Me? They were inviting *me* to spend time with them? I was their people? Words got stuck in my throat. I couldn't remember the last time I'd hung out with anyone who wanted to be friends with me that wasn't family.

"That sounds lovely, actually. I haven't been out in a long time. Should I bring something?" I asked.

"Only if you want to, but we've got it covered. Just bring yourself. Tell me, Regina." Lily leaned forward, resting her arms on her knees. "Have you always had the sight?"

A sigh rushed out of me. I played with my cuticles, which looked terrible compared to Lily and Katja's beautifully manicured nails. "Since I was a child, but I wasn't allowed to use it."

"Allowed?" Lily's eyebrows rose.

"I grew up in a strict home," I explained. "It's a lot to explain, but basically, anything to do with my psychic ability was discouraged. I spent many years pretending I couldn't see dead family members around the house."

"Ah. So, you don't only get impressions and information from people. You also see spirits?" Hearing Lily confirm it out loud made it sound less my imagination, more concrete.

"It sounds scarier than it is. They come to me for different reasons. Usually because they need help or want to communicate with loved ones, but since I was taught to turn them off, it doesn't go beyond that. Since I've been here, though..."

I was talking too much. I could feel the stares and scowls of all my family telling me to shut up.

"Yes?"

"Since I've been here, it's become stronger. I think it's the proximity to my birthplace, or maybe the ocean. Not sure. But it's stronger than ever. Like the other day when I picked up on your memories. I'm sorry again," I said to Katja.

"Don't apologize. You can't help what you see, and I still have work to do to exorcize that demon." She let loose a chuckle. "Anyway, I hope you don't mind that I shared the experience with Lily."

Lily nodded. "Seriously, we're all intuitive to some degree, but that's impressive. Have you had any impressions about this house?"

"Yes. There's a woman here named Vivian. She owned a cigar factory with her husband, but she handled the day-to-day operations in the very room you were talking about. Had a daughter named Nora."

"See?" Katja said when Lily's mouth dropped open.

"That I didn't know. The island records only indicate she had a son."

"And a daughter. Who left me flowers," I said. "Plumeria."

"Is that frangipani?" Lily asked.

"Yes."

Lily and Katja exchanged surprised looks. "Remember the night before you arrived, I said someone left flowers in the kitchen, which I thought was weird because the flowers were fresh but the house had been locked for months? Regina was the first person to stay here."

"That is super weird," Katja said. "Perfect backstory for your next *Dead & Breakfast*!"

Lily was staring at me in awe.

I didn't want to tell her anymore until I could be certain that Nora was, in fact, Vivian Montero's daughter. The screams and sounds of men shouting just a few minutes ago gave me a bad vibe, and I wanted to confirm the visions first.

"You have a real gift, Regina, one that could help people."

"Believe me, for years, I wanted to help people, but I couldn't. Maybe now that my husband's passed, and I've been spending time away from my son..." The tears were back, brimming at the edge of my lashes.

Lily reached out for my hand. "Maybe we can help you find yourself again. We're kind of good at that."

"She definitely needs to come to our next moon party," Katja said in a twangy version of her midwestern accent.

"Moon party?" I asked.

"Oh, you'll see." Katja winked and waved her hand like a magician making a dove disappear. "But shh...it's between us."

. . .

A secret society meeting.

I'd been invited to a secret meeting on my second week working for Lily Autumn for no other reason than because I had a little extra sensory perception. On one hand, I was excited to have what felt like possible friends, but on the other, I was terrified. Was my psychic ability the only reason they were being friendly?

No.

Lily Autumn had been kind from Day One and even Day Two, my first day on the job. Katja had been nice enough to introduce herself to me the day of the staff meeting, and that was before I blurted out the random SpongeBob comment. All that occurred before they knew anything about me. Simply put, these people were nice. Was that so hard to believe?

It was this thought, along with how tight jeans could get, that ran through my mind at work the next day when I saw Maya again. I could barely scrub a shower stall in my loose sweatpants, let alone bend and sweep underneath beds. How on Earth did she move in those? When we happened to cross paths in the same hallway, I pressed my back against the wall to give her plenty of space to pass. She wasn't a large girl, but her ego seemed to be getting bigger.

"I knew that was you," she said, stopping to straighten a vase I had straightened just a moment ago.

"What do you mean?"

"At the supermarket yesterday. You were behind me in the aisle, weren't you? Looking at candles? I was on the phone behind you? I noticed you when you walked away."

"Was I?" I played the fool. "I don't remember that."

There was no way to prove it'd been me listening in on

her conversation. It wasn't like I'd actively eavesdropped. She was the one talking loudly on speakerphone for any Tom, Dick, or *fulano* to hear. Besides, there had to be dozens of other unassuming middle-aged women with medium brown hair streaked with gray in the entirety of the supermarket. Was she going to suggest I knew her ulterior motive for being here? She couldn't make that suggestion without saying it again.

It was obviously the correct card to play. She had no way to call my bluff except for an extended stare with eyelids at half-mast. What was she going to do—ask me to keep her secret? That would require telling me her secret to begin with. No, as long as she didn't cross my path (besides in this hallway), I wouldn't throw her under the bus. I had nothing to gain by doing so. Work drama wasn't my game.

Stay out of my business, and I'll stay out of yours, I communicated with a simple look.

After a grueling day, I walked home in sweat-drenched clothes feeling every bit my advancing age. I hated to hate on Maya for her effortless youth, but I was feeling really old and resentful right now. How long would I be able to do this? Would I still be cleaning houses when I was over fifty? Without a perky body and Ariel the Mermaid face, how were new opportunities supposed to open up to a woman like me?

As much as Sid's words of empowerment had fueled me, they'd also saddened me. Higher positions didn't just happen for women like me. If, as a maid, I'd been invisible to begin with, even as a young woman, why would anyone take notice of me or give me opportunities now that I was practically a hag?

I wouldn't let it get me down. I'd heard of plenty of

people who'd gotten their start in career at a later age. Offhand, I couldn't think of anyone, but they existed. In the wild. Like Bigfoot or the Loch Ness Monster.

From the end of the street, behind the barricade, a group of young women and one young man called out and held up their phones. "Hi! Hey! Do you work for *Witch of Key Lime Lane?*" One of the girls tried flagging me down. "Do you know Lily Autumn? Can you tell her we love her for us?" They took photos of me, although for the life of me, I had no idea why.

"Is the Montero House really haunted?" another asked.

"We heard it is. The *Ghost Crew* says they plan on coming to investigate it."

"I, uh..." Had no idea who this ghost crew was, though I'd heard of them somewhere.

Our other security guard, Rick, drove his electric cart in from the periphery. "Guys, come on. I told you on the other street that you can't be here, okay? Thanks for dropping by. Keep watching the show. We'll let Lily know you were here." He shooed them away expertly, shook his head, and waved at me.

I thanked him with a nod.

When I walked through the door, I should've been surprised to see the capuchin waiting at the foot of the stairs, as though I owed him something. "How did you get in?" I asked.

I supposed, if he was going to make this a habit, I should give him a name. "Whatever. Stay as long as you want. I'm going to shower. Just make sure all the doors are closed. Okay, Mono?" It wasn't a particularly creative name, but it was accurate.

Mono chirped in confusion when I bypassed him on the stairs without a single offering for him. How dare I not transmute his underripe coconut into something delicious like I had his mango?

Suddenly, headlights beamed in through the window. Somebody had pulled up. Man, people really loved to visit when I was bone tired. But I also appreciated the attention, especially since it was Diego climbing out of his van. Someone must've spread the word on the island to make sure I did not go without friends.

I dropped back down two steps. "Ugh, and me looking like total shit." I pulled the elastic band out of my ponytail and ran fingers through my hair, trying to make magic out of mayhem.

"You know what? If he can't appreciate me looking like this, then it'll never work between us," I told Mono with a laugh.

I waited for the knock. No self-respecting lady would dare open the door to a gentleman caller before he had a chance to make his presence known. I was desperate, but not *that* desperate.

"Oh, hello," I said, as though I hadn't just watched him pull up, step out of the van, hurry up the walk, bound onto the patio, and stand outside my door for a full five seconds before I opened it.

Was it possible for a man to get even more sexy as time went by? Either my eyes were sorely in need of masculine beauty to behold, or Diego's magnificence had deepened in the days since I'd last seen him. He held out another container of ice cream and bowed.

"*Para ti*, milady. More coconut ice cream."

"*Muchísimas gracias, señor—*"

As I took the container from his hands, something tiny and human-like jumped onto my shoulder without warning. I squealed, realizing right away, of course, that it was Mono. "What are you—!"

Diego reached out while the corners of his mouth tightened into a suppressed smile. "He knows what's up. Come here, little one." He tried getting the monkey off my shoulder, but Mono swatted Diego's hand, then it was my turn to laugh at him. "Oh, is that how we're going to play?" Diego asked.

"Leave him, it's okay," I said. "He thinks I can turn whatever fruit he gives me into something even better."

"What did he give you last time?" Diego asked.

"Coconut."

"Then, it worked."

"It did," I said. Mono chirped so loudly, insisting I give him the ice cream, that I dropped his little body into the windowsill. "Sit, and I'll share."

To our surprise, Mono sat with his tiny hands folded in his lap and cocked his cute, monkey face.

"Good boy," I said. Removing the lid, I looked around for something to scoop, and Diego, predicting what I needed, reached into his shorts' pocket and pulled out a plastic spoon.

"I come prepared."

I let my eyebrows do the talking on this one.

"Thank you." I scooped coconut ice cream onto the marble windowsill and watched Mono dip his hands into the creamy deliciousness, lifting it into his mouth and smacking his little monkey lips together. "This creature is better at getting what it wants than I am," I said.

We stood there watching Mono eat, and I was thinking about manifestation and how some monkeys got all the luck when it hit me that I'd spoken aloud.

I looked at Diego.

"You're blushing." He smiled.

"I keep doing that. Making things sound weird."

"I like it. Makes you all the more genuine rather than unattainable."

I pushed my grimy hair back behind my ear. "Unattainable?" I scoffed. "Oh, yes. Look at the long line of men waiting for a chance at me outside this door."

But the moment I said it, I regretted it. In uttering such a self-deprecating remark, I'd simultaneously criticized his taste in women and put myself down as well. His dark eyes chastised me. His mouth opened to say something.

"What I mean is, thank you," I said. "I'm just not used to the attention. Sorry."

"Don't be. What I was going to tell you is that it's not that hard, getting what you want. Just ask. The universe is always listening."

"Yeah, well, it doesn't listen to me."

"Have you tried? What is it you want, Regina?"

Oof, the billion-dollar question everybody seemed to want me to answer. Should I tell him that I wanted my son back? That I wished I could start life all over and take advantage of the opportunities I'd been given while I still had them? Or fast forward to the part where I wished I could take command, for once, and invite this man upstairs into my bed despite being raised as a good girl who shouldn't wish for such pleasures?

"You don't want to hear my answer," I said.

"Actually, I do. Are you free tomorrow night?"

I froze.

I was getting asked on a date, something that never, ever happened to me. It felt alien and out of place, like happening at the wrong place and wrong time, twenty-five years too late. I knew that was fear, but it was all I could think.

Diego waited patiently, but then, he took something else out of his pocket—a quarter—and pretended to put it inside a slot by my ear.

"What are you doing?" I chuckled.

"Depositing another twenty-five cents. Seems my call has ended."

I laughed in quiet mortification. "'Your call is continuing,'" I tried on an operator's voice.

"Whew, thought I'd lost you for a minute."

I looked up at him. "I appreciate you asking me...very much." Though I did not, under any circumstances, want to dissuade this man from trying again in the future. "But, if it's okay with you, I will take a raincheck on that offer—for now."

I felt a myriad of emotions run through my heart—fear, embarrassment, surprise, disbelief—as he smiled and dipped his eyes. He did not seem hurt in any way. "Of course. But you will eat the rest of this ice cream yourself, right? I hate to think I brought it just for the primate."

Mono chirped.

"I promise." I dipped my finger into the ice cream and

popped it into my mouth, careful not to eye him or appear too seductive. "And I'll think of you as I do."

Whoa. Thoughts manifested into spoken word. Maybe I was becoming braver after all. Who was this strange woman speaking on my behalf? Mono stared at us like watching a ping-pong match.

Luminous bits of amusement sparkled in Diego's eyes, as he handed me his *Sweet Spot* business card. "Fair enough, Regina. Here, take this...for whenever you're ready."

ten

FOR DAYS, I couldn't fall asleep right away.

I'd lay in bed, staring at the ceiling, feeling the breezy heat of a dying South Florida winter. Most people might remedy insomnia with melatonin or lavender tea, but each night, I'd use the spirit board again and again in search of answers that might help me nod off.

Each night, I'd talk to Nora, even though it was Pablito I wanted, and each night I'd hear screams throughout the house, echoing from a distant place, followed by shouts of men angry about land, broken promises, and false deeds. At times, I'd hear the vintage Cuban music playing again or the sounds of *el lector* reading aloud in the factory. I'd ask Nora if she was alright, if there was anything she needed to tell me, but I never got answers. It felt like whatever tragic event happened here was replaying itself over and over in an infinite loop. Eventually, I'd end up in the bathroom on the verge of throwing up.

On the third night, I found flowers again. This time, they were on my nightstand. I lifted them to my nose and inhaled the scent of plumeria, as tears rose into my eyes. All my life, I rarely got flowers, except from my children. Daniel wasn't the type to buy them for me, always saying they were a waste of money, preferring practical gifts like a blender or a hand vacuum. Sure, we needed those, but they weren't romantic or befitting of a woman who'd worked her ass off all day. And now here, this wisp of a girl ghost was leaving them for me.

"Thanks, Nora."

I broke into a fresh round of tears. I was tired of crying. Tears had become my everyday companion, but they were greedy, taking up so much of my energy. What about smiles? What about laughter? Didn't they want equal space in my life? The only way out of this endless cycle, I realized, was to start doing things differently, find a way out of my comfort zone.

Dumping the old dead flowers in the trash, I replaced the glass with the fresh blooms, set them on my nightstand, and fell asleep.

The night of the full moon party, I stepped onto the front veranda wearing an old green sundress, holding a bottle of wine I'd bought for myself earlier in the week with the intention of drinking away my pain. I'd never gotten around to doing that, since working myself to death was my preferred pain management method. I was half-hoping to find Diego bounding up the steps to bring me some delicious new flavor of ice cream, but it was probably a good sign that he wasn't there after I'd rejected him. It would suck if he turned out to be a stalker who couldn't take no for an answer.

Before leaving, I placed two bowls on the porch for Mono, one with water, one with scraps of leftovers. I didn't know whose monkey he was or whether feeding a wild monkey was acceptable, but I needed to feel like someone needed me.

I arrived at a house next to Lily's decorated with fairy lights, rainbow mobiles, and flowers. From the moment I stepped onto the property, I felt a warm, loving aura wrap around me. Whatever went on here on the daily contained healing energy for sure. The door opened as though the house had been expecting me, and one of the women I'd seen around before stepped out in a yellow caftan, looking like a disco-era African goddess wearing golden bangles and auburn hair in a big poof at the back of her head.

"Hello, my lovely! We've been waiting for you." She came down the steps and wrapped me in a light, welcoming hug. "I'm Heloise."

"Regina. Nice to meet you. I brought this." I handed her the wine bottle awkwardly, realizing I'd bought one of the cheap, twist-off cap kind, which I knew was a fancy party faux pas. Hopefully, this wasn't fancy.

Heloise did not seem like the type to mind. "Thank you!" she said as though I'd selected the finest grapes. "We're just waiting on Lily. You know how that is."

"Always late, that one is," another woman said. She appeared from the kitchen wearing jean shorts, a tank top, and muddy eyeliner around bright eyes, and to be honest, her bluntness intimidated me.

"This is my wife, Jeanine," Heloise said.

"Pleased to meet you." I gave into Jeanine's strong cigarette-scented hug. For a home with a smoker living in it, it smelled pretty nice in here. "What is that?" I sniffed the air.

"Isn't it lovely? It's a Japanese sandalwood," Heloise said.

I was referring to something delicious on the stove, but I nodded and took in the delightful décor of the home, an interesting blend of Asian sculpture, Indian tapestries, and psychedelic wall art. In the middle of one wall was a large, colorful painting of a flower unfurling that could easily be misinterpreted as a woman's vagina. The more I stared at it, however, the more I realized that was probably the artist's intention.

"That's Heloise's pussy painting. Makes you hungry, doesn't it? I'll go check the shrimp." Jeanine walked away.

"Geez, Jeanine, you're going to scare her away on the first visit." Katja slid in from the backyard, holding a beer. "Hey, Regina. Don't mind her."

Heloise shook her head, as she led me through the house to the backyard. "Yes. It's like a hazing ritual for her, to say the most embarrassing things she can just to see who can stand her."

"I heard that," Jeanine said.

"Your home is beautiful," I said. All around were trees and more trees, suspended twinkling lights, garden mushroom sculptures, wooden benches, pinwheels, and flowers, as though their backyard had been decorated by forest nymphs.

"Thank you! Ah, there she is," Heloise said.

My boss arrived, walking in alongside the young man I'd seen at *House of Dolls*, an androgynous fellow with piercing blue eyes and a cool, wide-brimmed hat. At once, he seemed out of place with all these older ladies but fit right in as well.

For a while, we chatted and made small talk, ate appetizers prepared by Jeanine and Heloise and mini key lime bites made by Lily herself. "You should've seen the first time I made a key lime pie, Reggie. I was so proud. I brought it here thinking I'd make these conchs proud, but they laughed at me."

"What's a conch?" I asked.

"People from the Keys," Katja said. "You're where I was a year ago." She smiled.

"We did not laugh at you, sweetheart," Heloise balked. "We accepted the dessert with open minds and hearts."

"We totally laughed at her," Jeanine said. "It was awesome. Here was this big-time, know-it-all New York City chef who piled merengue on top of a gelatin base of...something...I don't know what...and called it key lime pie. And for once, I knew something some expert didn't."

Everyone laughed, even me. "Rookie mistake."

Lily sipped from her glass of wine. "I tell you, I've learned so much living in the Keys. You're from South Florida, right?"

Here came the part where I was expected to talk about myself with four pairs of eyes looking at me. "Mostly. I came from Cuba when I was three. My parents died bringing me here..."

"Oh, no," Katja said. "I did not know that. I'm so sorry."

"No worries, it was a long time ago."

"You grew up with close relatives?" Lily asked.

"Friends of the family," I answered. "All my direct family stayed in Cuba. I've never met them in person. We just hear from them every couple of years."

"Would you want to visit them?" Heloise asked.

I shook my head. I had no desire to go back to a place that

put my parents' lives and my own in danger, no matter how beautiful it was. For refugees in the U.S., Cuba would remain nothing but a distant memory.

"I understand that," Heloise said. "Sometimes you have to leave the past where it belongs."

"Amen to that," Jeanine said, lighting up what looked like a joint. Forty-seven years, and I'd managed never to see anyone smoking one in person.

"Babe." Heloise gave her an embarrassed look.

"What? It's not a big deal. Is it a big deal?" she asked everyone. "I mean, can we all stop pretending it's a big deal? What year is this again?"

I laughed. "I'm okay with it, seriously." I mean, this was her own home. She could do whatever the heck she wanted.

The kid named Sam didn't speak much, but he did start up a fire in the firepit, as we all sat around drinking, talking, and eating while he poked at the wood and sent embers floating into the air. Such a beautiful night. Such beautiful people. They were complete strangers, yet I felt like I'd known them forever, like we'd been family in another lifetime.

It made me realize just how much I'd always been the black sheep of Daniel's family with my occult-like tendencies and inability to comprehend why they did things the way they did. Maybe now that I wasn't there as much anymore, they could finally breathe a sigh of relief that their resident weirdo wasn't around to embarrass them.

After a glass of wine, I eased in a bit more and found myself opening up, telling them things I never told anyone, except for maybe Pablito, because my son had been cut from the same cloth as I had when it came to beating his own drum. It was his curiosity that had led him to seeking new friendships, which ultimately led to his being in the wrong place at the wrong time.

Before I knew it, I was sobbing with Heloise next to me, patting my arm, and Lily cross-legged at my feet, and Katja and Sam leaning on each other watching me with empathy.

"Oh, honey, it's no wonder you're in the space that you are," Lily said. "But you didn't cause your son's passing. You know that, don't you?"

I couldn't respond, because I wasn't sure of that.

"For all we know, that boy was meant to live a short life. It might've been set from the beginning; you just didn't know it. He was here to experience being human and bring joy to you while doing it. I'm so sorry, sweetheart." Heloise continued to pat my hand with her bright, orange nails. "But it wasn't your fault."

I cleared my eyes, breathed in deeply, and let it out. "I guess I needed to talk about it," I said. "You'd be surprised how quickly everyone expects a person to get over death and move on."

"That's because it's hard for them to see you in pain, but you take as long as you need. And if you want to come here and talk about it all you want, our door is always open." Coming from Jeanine, that meant a lot. What a lovely invitation.

"Honestly, I probably won't. I'm tired of grieving, of waiting for things to change. I know I shouldn't say this with my boss sitting right here, but I'm tired of busting myself for everyone else."

"I get that," Lily said. "Believe me, I do."

"Nothing to do with work," I said, eyeing her. "I just wish

things would happen for me, for once, as easily as they happen for other people, if that makes sense."

"Total sense."

"Perfect sense."

"You need luck," Sam said.

Everyone looked at him.

I nodded. "Just a break would be nice. I think that's what it is. I think I'm just tired. Exhausted—mentally, physically, emotionally—in every way imaginable." I looked around to see four earnest faces watching me, listening, really listening. But I did not come here to be their downer. That was another thing I was tired of—making people sad when they saw me.

No more.

I rolled back my shoulders. "I'm actually really glad you invited me here, Lily, Katja... Because for a while now, I've felt like I'm on the brink of something, on the precipice of something bigger, you know? Maybe that's wishful thinking, but there has to be more."

"There is more," Katja assured.

"I know that feeling, too." Lily took my hands. "It's the uncertainty that sits with you a bit, right before you start a new life. We can help with that. Can't we, witches?" Four faces exploded into big smiles.

eleven

TWO DAYS LATER, I was still thinking about that evening. Because of that "hangout," my time spent cleaning day in, day out, felt lighter. The way they'd rallied around me, the decision to pray for me, only they didn't call it praying, but it was praying just the same. A "luck spell," they'd called it where Sam fetched a dried palm frond, Lily handed me a Sharpie, and Heloise asked me to write five things I wanted to ask the universe for.

When I looked at her questioningly, she said, "Or God. Girl, we don't discriminate here. This works no matter who you're dealing with—the Universe, the Goddess, Hecate, Santa Muerte, your spirit guides...whoever you want. That's the beauty of the craft, you make it your own."

I chose to ask God and the Universe for freedom from having to constantly look for work, a break from physical labor, and acceptance to know that my son was at peace. I wrote them on the dried palm frond.

"That's only three," Jeanine had said.

"That's all I want," I'd replied. If they thought I was

going to ask for millions of dollars, that wasn't who I was. I'd tried to focus on what mattered most.

Shaking her head, "Okay, then..." Jeanine had me repeat a mantra over and over. I still had it memorized: *Luck comes to me. Abundance is my birthright. I attract money and opportunities.*

We all closed our eyes, and they joined me, as we surrounded the bonfire. I was supposed to repeat the mantra until I could visualize it, believe it, internalize it, and I'll be honest—I couldn't feel it. Not like I knew I was supposed to. It felt good to know that other people were rooting for me.

If only I could root for myself.

Still, it'd been a magical night, as we tossed the palm frond into the fire and watched it burn, the smoke curling up toward the heavens, carrying my request with it. As we sat there, chanting this mantra that eventually turned into a little song, I crossed my fingers and hoped that they would invite me again some other time. The evening had been a lot like church, except the palmetto trees were the church walls, the bonfire was the altar, and the stars were the prayer candles.

When I'd gotten home, I'd found a sleepy monkey sitting on my porch, as though he'd been waiting for me all night. The food I'd left him was replaced with three small, yellow-green key limes.

"Do I look like a magician to you?"

He'd chirped and rolled a lime toward my foot.

I'd sighed. "I'll see what I can do. Goodnight."

· · ·

Next day, I was walking to work, beachside, as I usually did, three weeks into working at *Dead & Breakfast* and really starting to enjoy these morning walks, especially when I got to see Diego. I still hadn't had a "beach day," but every day, I looked forward to my commune with seagulls, sandpipers, guests out for a stroll, and Diego setting up his cart.

Today, however, Diego wasn't there. I felt disappointed not seeing him, even though I'd shot him down at every turn. Even though he only sold ice cream three times a week, I felt, while standing in his spot thinking about his dimply smile, that perhaps he wouldn't be coming by as often anymore. The thought made me sad. I spent the day thinking about a world without Diego in it, even though I'd made it abundantly clear to him I wasn't ready to date.

When Mono had handed me fruit, he'd fully expected it to become ice cream. Was it coincidence or the little monkey's faith that manifested his desires? I couldn't help but wonder if my keeping distance from Diego had actively pushed him away, if my standoffish energy had repelled him. If so, I had to somehow change that. If I let my stupid fears guide my every move, I would never manifest the things I'd asked for on that palm frond last night.

I managed to keep my distance from Maya today, though I had to say, she talked to too many fans lined up behind the barricades when we weren't supposed to encourage them. She also held Katja hostage in the living room a whole five minutes asking her detailed questions about the show they were in the middle of taping. Was the pay nice? Did she know Lily Autumn would choose her for a hostess? Did she have any idea what Lily would look for in the next host, assuming there would be a next show?

Qué pena! No shame. She may as well have worn a sign on her forehead—*Ask me about my ulterior motive.*

In the evening, Captain Jax, Lily's beau, and Sid drove past the house in a golf cart to check out the patching and sanding they'd done on the exterior of the porch. Both waved at me and made small talk, but it was Diego I was truly wishing would stop by to drop off ice cream or chat with me. Even Mono waited with bated breath, hoping fresh key lime dessert would magically appear after leaving me a few.

When the sun sank below the dark purple clouds on the other side of the island, I showered, sat on the porch with a glass of wine, for once, and asked myself: How terrible would it be? If I went into my purse and fished out Diego's business card, and called him? Would it be a betrayal of my husband? Of my family? Of the woman I used to be? Whenever I'd ever heard about women asking men out on dates, part of me never believed I could do that. Another part of me... To be so bold. To go for what you want.

Enough.

I flew into the house, found the business card, and sat on the porch, phone in hand. "He's just a person. Call him, Reggie, for crying out loud. He's just a man."

That helped to de-mystify the ice cream vendor quite a bit, especially when I imagined that he would be delighted to hear from me, when I envisioned myself as a powerful, sexy being myself.

When I got his voicemail, part of me was relieved he didn't answer, and I was about to leave a simple message, when suddenly, his number was calling me back at the same time.

"Hey," I said.

"Hello. Who am I speaking with again? Sorry, I some-times forget to save my clients' numbers..." We'd never had a phone conversation before, so there was no reason for him to have my number saved.

I held my breath. "It's Regina. From the Montero House? *Dead & Breakfast?*"

The longest moment went by. I could practically see the gears in his head turning to remember which of the tens of thousands of women who flirted with him daily was Regina, *Regina, Regina...*

Maybe I should hang up.

"Re-*hee*-na," he said in a long, sexy Spanish drawl. "So nice to hear from you. Are you calling on your own behalf or that of your fiendish ice-cream-loving monkey?"

I laughed. "Myself."

"Ah, very nice."

I closed my eyes, inhaled a deep breath... *No pain, no gain.* And just said the words, "That raincheck...can I redeem it soon?"

I imagined him leaning back in bed, smiling. "I thought you'd never ask."

He picked me up on my next day off, and like he'd asked me to, I'd worn a swimsuit underneath my shorts and tank top, because when in Rome and all that. Nothing unusual about sportswear 'round these parts, but I hadn't worn a swimsuit in ages, and I was self-conscious about the cellulite on the back of my thighs. Years of grueling physical work had kept me in relatively good shape, but I'd always felt weird about my small breasts and boyish body.

What I hadn't expected was to see Diego show up on a motorized scooter. Did that mean I'd have to sit behind him, spread my knees to accommodate him between my legs, and wrap my arms around his solid waist with my hands clasped around his tight abs? Yes, it did. Diego was at least six feet tall, if not more. My husband had been five-nine and slight. I didn't mean to compare, but I couldn't help it. I'd never wrapped my arms around another man who wasn't a grown boy of my own before.

I was already thinking this to be a bad idea, that I wouldn't be able to fake being the confident woman I desperately wanted to be, like Katja the first day I saw her, when I reminded myself to have fun.

Enjoy it, Reg.

All was fair in love and war until we pulled into a parking lot where the sign very clearly read "Ocean Adventures," and just like that, doubt settled in and good feelings were gone.

"Where are we going?" I shouted over the motor.

"Swimming with dolphins!" he shouted back, swerving through the parking lot.

"Oh, no, Diego. I don't...I don't think so." The moment we parked, I explained, "I don't like the ocean. I probably should've told you when you asked me to wear a bathing suit, but I was thinking we'd sit on the beach, not swim."

"You don't swim?" he asked.

"I do. I swim in pools and wade in the shallow surf just fine. I just...I'm scared of the ocean. When I was little..." My words melted into the boiling hot blacktop. How many times would I repeat this story as an excuse not to try something new?

He hopped off the scooter and turned around in his seat,

facing me, brown eyes across from mine. "It won't be the ocean. It's a contained reservoir. Perfectly safe. We can leave if you want to. I respect that, but just telling you—"

I felt an old ball of nerves tightening up inside my stomach.

"I know these people. They do a fantastic job. They even help children with all sorts of anxieties. Is that okay?"

I had to try, or I would never budge from this place of fear, and I was so very tired of being there.

"Trust me," he said.

And maybe because I desperately wanted to trust him, or because I was tired of sheltering, protecting, and making excuses for my fear, I nodded. For once, it'd be nice to let someone else take care of me.

twelve

THE FOLKS at Ocean Adventures were, like Diego said, amazing. First, we took a short class that went over dolphin basics. We learned that most swim-with-the-dolphin attractions were actually not great for the dolphins, which surprised me, because I thought that was why we were there. I learned that none of the dolphins at Ocean Adventures had been bred in captivity nor were they wild, healthy dolphins that should've been freely swimming in the ocean. All of them had been injured in some way and thus were living here in a conservatory. Basically, they'd been given a second chance at life.

I also learned that a dolphin's natural curve of its mouths made people believe that they were always good-natured creatures, but they weren't always. They got into foul moods just like people did. They could get stressed, angry, and aggressive, so we should never assume they were always friendly. The idea here was to interact slowly, to pick up their energy, as they picked up yours, and to form a bond based on trust.

These dolphins were never forced to perform nor interact with humans, so they weren't stressed out of their minds like at other facilities. We were invited to hang out in the large, supervised pen, and if the dolphins wanted to interact with you, that was up to them. If they didn't, that was fine, too, but there was no guarantee of an interaction, even with a paid session.

When it was time to get in the water, I nearly couldn't do it. I knew it was an enclosed area of natural ocean water, and I knew there was little to no chance of drowning with so many lifeguards supervising, but tell that to my PTSD brain. All I kept seeing was the starburst shape of the sun through the water, as I sank, lower, lower, lower into the ocean...

"You okay?" Diego asked, offering his hand to help me step to the platform's edge, again when he jumped in the water, and again when he invited me in.

Any normal woman would've noticed the moment he stripped off his shirt, donned flippers, and dove into the water, but I was so busy being terrified of breathing H2O instead of air that I barely noticed Diego until he was extending his hand up for me to join him. "It's okay. I got you."

Despite my hesitation, I jumped in with flippers and immediately began to tread water, trying to think of all the positive sensations I was experiencing—sun on my cheeks, the warmth of the water, the strength of Diego's tanned fore-arms and the way he kept swishing back his dark hair to keep it out of his eyes and blowing small bursts of water every time he dipped below the surface.

"You doing good?"

"I'm okay." Eventually, I felt confident enough to swim

around the enclosure, holding onto the rocky, grassy edges, my eyes peeled for dorsal fins splitting the surface.

"They won't let the dolphins out yet," he explained, pushing my hair behind my ears. It was a very loving gesture that made me wonder if Diego had children. "Not until everyone feels comfortable."

"I'm not scared of the dolphins," I said. "More scared of going under. It's irrational, I know." I'd given Diego the low-down on my fear based on my childhood experience prior to the class starting, so he knew where I was coming from. "Do you have kids? I feel like you would make a good dad. 'Cause you seem really understanding."

When Diego smiled, it seemed like the whole enclosure lit up with it. And there was something primal about him that made my stomach do somersaults.

"I don't have kids," he said to my surprise.

"Really? I never would've guessed."

"We just never had any."

We? A small surge of panic shot through my chest. Was I swimming with a married man? I didn't care if he was estranged, that would not work for me, no way, no how.

He gave a small laugh. "Sorry, that sounded wrong. I meant 'we,' as in my ex and I—long time ago. It just never happened. I always wanted kids, but..." His words trailed off, and a melancholy slipped in.

"Sorry. Didn't meant to dredge up the past. Was just curious, that's all."

"No worries. What about you? Kids?"

"Two boys. Had," I corrected, closing my eyes, focusing on the warm rays of sun burning my cheeks. "Lost one three years ago."

"Damn, Regina, I'm so sorry. What happened?" I felt the light tug of his fingers pulling on mine under the water.

"DUI. The car flew a hundred feet. Hit a palm tree."

He covered his face with his hands. It was usually difficult for people to hear the story. Me, I just felt more and more numb each time I told it, like it happened to someone else, and I was just a better narrator every time.

"How old?"

"Twenty-five," I replied, followed by a moment of silence. "Then, my husband passed seven months ago, so it's been a rough time for me. Anyway, now you know why I'm such a spaz."

"A spaz?" He scoffed. "You are the total opposite of a spaz, Reggie. Anyone else would've given up after what you've been through. You? You keep going. I see you every other day, working your butt off, smiling as you go..."

"I don't 'smile as I go'." I laughed and probably smiled.

"You do. It's the first thing I noticed about you," he said. "You smile as you walk to and from work. You have this outlook about you, like the world's not going to collapse under your feet, not if you can help it."

"The truth is I'm just trying to hold it together."

"I think you're stronger than you give yourself credit for. You really do keep your chin up. Made me wonder what secrets you're hiding underneath that façade. Do you want to try one of the exercises?"

During class, they'd suggested partnering up and taking turns floating while the other person lightly held them from underneath. Team building trust exercise and all that. "Sure. What do I do again?"

"Float on your back like you did when you were five years old learning to swim," Diego said.

That was the problem. When I thought of floating in the water, I was always three years old and felt out of control, too small and weak for the powers of the riptide. This time, without currents to suck me underneath, and with Diego here to make sure I was safe, I allowed myself to feel that way.

I leaned back, holding my arms out wide. Diego's skin felt nice against mine, and even though my brain wanted to overanalyze everything—whether he was checking out my body as I floated, whether I'd shaved my bikini line close enough, whether I should wait longer before dating, whether I still looked desirable or too old, whether he might expect more from me after this—I steered my thoughts into a new direction.

I feel safe.

I am safe with this person who cares about me.

This feels nice.

I feel happy and free.

I was even imagining what it might feel like to get even closer to Diego, to allow myself some happiness—not now but later on, once we got to know each other better—what his shoulders might feel like with my arms around them, what his scent might be if I leaned in and allowed myself to breathe him in, what his lips might feel like...when I sensed something bump my ankles.

My eyes shot open.

Diego smiled. "It's okay. We have a visitor. I got you."

He indeed had me, arms locked underneath my planked body, firmly keeping me from harm. I would not be sinking or drowning today. I got bumped again, this time on my left leg, and when a smooth, long body brushed up against my hand, a flood of memories hit me so hard, I was overwhelmed with emotion.

"Reg? You're okay." Diego's voice emanated concern, as his thumb swiped my lower lids.

I was crying. Of course, I was crying, because trauma took time to heal, but also because that smooth body, that rubbery skin I'd never touched before, felt exactly the same as the one in my dreams of drowning. Each time I sank lower, as my lungs burned, and the starburst of sun in the ocean's ceiling got smaller and smaller, a smooth warm body just like this one, pushed me up higher and higher.

My angel...

Then, I'd reach the ocean ceiling. Then, I'd see the arms, the raft, the people's faces, hear their shouts in Spanish to hurry up and grab me. Underneath me, my angel would push me upwards, an angel with a rubbery snout...

Pushing me...like a beach ball...

"It was a dolphin," I muttered.

Diego leaned his ear closer to my lips. "What's that?"

"A dolphin," I said, stepping out of his hold.

As I tread water and looked for our cetacean friend, I wasn't sure what I was saying even made sense, so I didn't elaborate, but Diego thought I meant the dolphin that was here with us now, playfully, shyly acknowledging us and swimming off.

"Yep, there he is. Hey, buddy!"

But the more I thought about it, the more it made sense. The angel from the depths, the one that saved me that day, the day I nearly drowned forty-four years ago out in the waters between Cuba and Miami, hadn't been my imagination from my post-trauma dreams. It hadn't been an angel, at least not the kind with wings and a cherubic face. It'd been a mammal—a wild, ocean creature with the intelligence to know that another creature was drowning and needed help.

It was a dolphin—

—a dolphin saved my life.

"Did you have a good day?" Standing on my porch, watching me insert the key, Diego bit his upper lip nervously. "I feel like I made you do something you didn't want to do."

I thought back on the day—swimming with our dolphin, holding onto his dorsal fin, going for a short ride. Our dolphin wasn't particularly feeling too sociable, which was perfect for me. Slow and steady wins the race. Afterwards, we ate lunch at the facility's cafeteria out by the water, then drove up and down the islands on Diego's scooter, soaking up the sun.

"No, it was great," I assured him. "Seriously, don't feel bad. This? What we did today? It was so good for me."

He smiled, cranked back his elbows, and knocked an imaginary ball out of the park. "That is a wonderful thing to hear."

"Yeah, it was." I opened the door and nervously hovered there. What was one supposed to do after a date? A long time ago, a kiss would've been expected, but we were well into the 21st century now and the thought of kissing Diego both intrigued and terrified me.

What if he expected more?

What if I liked it?

What if my husband and son could see me from the other side?

What if that was just an excuse because the truth was, I'd never kissed anyone other than Daniel and part of me was scared I might want more? Was Diego even a good man to start over with? Wouldn't starting a romantic situation now be a bit like going from the frying pan into the fire?

I smiled at Diego and took his hand, keeping my gaze down on it the whole time, because looking into his eyes would feel too intense.

"Hey. You don't owe me anything, Reg. I had a nice time." He sensed my hesitation and rubbed my knuckles with his thumb. "Okay?"

I nodded.

He wrapped both arms around me and gave me a nice hug. Not too deep, not creepy, just enough to let me know that he had a nice time today, that we were good no matter how fast or slow I wanted this to progress.

"How much do I owe you, at least? A dollar amount. I'm the one who called you."

He shook his head. "It was nothing."

"Don't say that. Let me pay for part of it."

He shook his head again. "I said no, woman."

"But I'll feel like I owe you." I cocked my head. "And you said I don't owe you."

"That..." He pointed at me, raising his eyebrows. "Is not going to work."

"Fine. I'll buy ice cream from you then, next time I see you," I said.

"Fair enough. I'll see you soon." He backed away and

hopped down the steps. "Which, by the way, might be once or twice a week from now on. More clients on the way." He waved.

I watched him stroll over to his scooter, start it up, and drive down the street as the sun started going down. I let out the biggest sigh. I might've resisted Diego today, but I knew I wouldn't be able to resist him for long.

thirteen

DROPPING, down, down into the sea.

Lungs burning, starburst rotating high above me, arms flailing, as waters grew chillier, then colder. Down, down, darker and deeper. So alone in the vast emptiness. Nothing but suspended particles for companions.

A pinprick of light opened up, like the eye of a predator or a lens shutter. Wider, calling me home. Calling me to the step through, leave this world behind, return to the cosmos. Love was there. Light was there. Light so comforting, without pain, without struggle ever again. I wanted to go to the light, but I was on the precipice again.

More.

There was something more.

I was here for more, but what?

Not ready.

The angel knew.

The angel swept in from the darkness and pushed me upwards. I floated higher, as it bumped me higher, upwards, toward the ocean ceiling. Floated up. Bumped me like a ball.

Leaving darkness behind, slowly rising like a balloon into the air. The angel nudged my elbow, wedged itself into my armpit and urged me to go higher. On the surface was the raft. I was afraid of the raft. I'd fallen from the raft, and returning to the raft meant slipping from men's hands again and plummeting again.

No.

Let me die.

Another voice. *You are not ready.*

Seemed I was never ready. Not on land, not at sea, not deep under the ocean. What was I waiting for? I was an older woman, for God's sake, or was I still a child in this dream? Either way, I was tired of this in-between state, suspended like plankton waiting to be eaten. I knew I was dreaming and just wanted to wake up.

Wake up. You're not dying.

At least I was aware this time and wasn't afraid.

Finally, my head broke the surface, and I sucked in a deep rush of air, as people around me made a big fuss, and I lay on the raft, gasping like a fish, staring into the water at the gray, silvery missile that had propelled me. Now it slipped away like an anchor dropped into the fathoms.

Thank you, I told the creature.

Then, sitting with me on the raft was Vivian Montero. Nobody saw her, but I did. They flipped me over, administered CPR, swaddled me in towels, but all I saw was Vivian Montero, the sun a swollen halo of light around her head, crying like a Virgin of Guadalupe.

The men came, she said.

What men? I remembered the men her daughter had mentioned as well.

They searched for our money, they killed my daughter. They took her livelihood, her dreams. They burned it all.

Burned? But her house hadn't been burned, as far as I knew. I tried to tell her this. I actually tried to argue with a dream spirit that she was mistaken about her own life. What made me so sure? The hurricane came shortly after, she said. The destruction, the loss of life, it'd all been blamed on the hurricane. Nobody knew the truth.

Which is? I asked.

It was the men, the men who destroyed everything. She reached down and lifted the bauble around my neck, which had fallen to the side and rested on its chain on the raft's half-rotted wood. *Have you seen my husband?* she asked again.

I haven't. I'm sorry, I replied, same as I had the first time she asked me that question, but this ghost was programmed to ask, and I wasn't even sure she knew it was me, the same lady she'd asked last time.

I saved my son, she said. I hadn't even known she had a son. *Before I walked into the sea, I gave him away.*

God, her sadness—I felt it like intravenous meds pulsing through my veins, reaching every part of my soul, informing every organ and every limb, so that I might know her pain. But I didn't need to familiarize her pain—I had my own, and maybe that was why she was drawn to me. I just never knew Vivian had taken her own life.

I'm so sorry. May I ask you a question? What about my son? I dared ask. If she was on the other side, she might see him. She might be able to put this mother's grief to rest. *Have you seen Pablito?*

Have you seen him? she answered my question with her own, hands wringing in worry. *Have you seen my husband?*

Ugh, we would never get anywhere like this.

"No," I spoke aloud with much more clarity. "I haven't. I'm sorry." My eyes opened. I was on the beach at night again. Sleeping. Sleepwalking? Dark purple clouds roiled on a red horizon; waves churned toward the shore. My fingertips touched the charm on the chain around my neck, but I never seemed to find comfort in it.

Why did I wear it?

I heard the screams, and not just Nora's but everyone's. I turned my bare feet around in the sand, facing north, and spotted the men coming for me. Angry, wanting their money, money someone had not delivered to them in time, and now that person would pay the price. Civilized men, but angry like pirates.

I stumbled, jumped to my feet, as they came toward me, except I wasn't me—I was somebody else. A man. I wore a guayabera, a hat, and in my pocket were two cigars, a roll of cash, and a cigar pick. I know because the men reached me, pummeled me with their fists, took the sharp, pointy cigar pick from my pocket...

Let's see if she can survive without him, one of them laughed, and impaled my broad chest with it.

I struggled to breathe, woke up screaming in bed. In the house. Not on the beach. I was safe. It wasn't me—it was Vivian's husband, Ramón. "Geez," I murmured, smelling plumeria on the breeze.

In my hand was the bauble I'd ripped off my neck in real life, off the chain, snapped it right off during the struggle with myself. Except, it wasn't a bauble at all. I recognized it now. It was the head of a cigar pick, broken off. And it'd once belonged to Vivian Montero's missing husband.

. . .

For a week, I slept with the light on.

I stayed away from the bauble after researching on my phone and learning that cigar picks often had ornate heads made to resemble animal heads, fleurs de lis, globes, all sorts of designs. Sometimes they were just round or pyramid-shaped with intricate, carved details in them. That same morning, early before the workers arrived, I'd taken the metallic piece into the cigar factory room where they were installing a new floor.

"I saw him," I told Vivian, wherever she happened to be. I knew she could hear me. "I saw your husband on the beach. He didn't disappear. They murdered him. I'm sorry."

I gave her the bauble, pressing it into a knot of fresh-cut underflooring wood. I didn't know the rest of the story, but I was guessing they took him to sea and dumped his body. Maybe that was how the broken tip of his cigar pick had washed ashore seventy years later when I happened to be standing there. Either way, I brought it home to her, where it belonged, but the moment I walked away, something called me back.

I stared at the bauble pressed into the wood, knowing if I left it there, the workers would cover it up, and there it would remain for another hundred years. But it was a cursed object, and cursed objects should be destroyed. Running over to it, I picked it back up and took it back to my room, placing it next to Pablito's Captain America T-shirt.

During the week, Diego brought key lime ice cream, and Mono did ecstatic cartwheels over it, as he and I talked on the porch for an hour (the man, not the monkey). After which, we texted quite a bit, but I didn't see him on the beach with his cart. Sometimes he'd try calling in the middle of the day while I was at work, but I always had to call him back later. For someone who understood what it meant to work day in, day out for pay, he sure didn't understand the concept of available hours.

But the distraction was turning out to be good for me. I was tired of dealing with Maya, who was talking behind my back every chance she got. At one point, I heard her telling the other girl that I was obsessed with the occult stuff in the house. I mean, of course I was. The crystals and geodes, spirit boards, stemware, dinnerware, elaborately painted Gothic dolls were works of art that anyone would admire, even someone who wasn't into creepy things, and if she wanted to be on TV as a future host of Lily's show, she had better learn to love them, too.

At one point, I caught her talking to a couple of fans waiting at the barricade, heard the words "ghost crew" again leave her lips, and as much as I wanted to know what she was talking about, I was raised to mind my own business. When I reached Mango Road, I asked Serge, who finally gave me a clue, "She's friends with some YouTubers on Key Largo called the *Ghost Crew*," he explained. "Dudes that investigate abandoned and haunted places."

"Ah," I said. "And she's on the show?"

"I don't think so, but they're friends, so she promotes them."

"Gotcha. Thanks," I said, walking to the Montero House, waving at old Mrs. Patisse who was grabbing the mail from her mailbox.

Yes, Diego gave me someone to talk to for longer than a

few minutes, and in the last few days, our texts had turned slightly sexy. No sexting—that wasn't my style—but lots of flirting that eventually led to the exchange of a few selfies. In Diego's last one, I could see his bathroom behind him, and dang, if that wasn't a nice bathroom.

Cleanest bathroom I've ever seen, I texted. For whatever strange reason, I'd pictured him living in a small, untidy, old house.

My mama raised me right, he replied.

The next evening, while he was busy catering for an evening island wedding, I took a walk to Lily's house. She'd called earlier in the day to see how I was doing and had told me about another "moon party" at Heloise's. This one was in celebration of the full moon tonight, and worried about mixing pleasure with business, I'd told her I might be too tired.

But there was nothing to do in this half-renovated, empty mansion full of ghosts, and I was thinking I might try reaching Pablito again with the spirit board when I remembered Jeanine asking a question during our get-together— Would we ever do a group séance?

I had stayed quiet on the matter, but now that I thought about it, there was no reason not to. The six of us had a great bond, and if anyone could pull it off successfully, it was us —*the island witches,* I thought with a laugh.

Walking up to Heloise and Jeanine's, I found a note on the door that said they were on the beach, further away from the guest areas. I made an about-face and headed down the steps, but I didn't feel right cutting through Lily or Jax's properties, so I headed back out Key Lime Lane with the intention of turning into the next street and walking all the way down to the beach. I wasn't expecting to see the contractor truck parked in an empty lot, nor the tangle of hands and feet pressed against the windshield, nor the moans of ecstasy muffled inside the sealed cab.

I walked quickly, trying not to be seen, but out of the corner of my eye, I could see it was Katja and her man, Evan, going at it pretty heavily like teenagers at Lookout Point. There was something raw and primal about it, something carnal and full of energy, the way she sat astride him, one strap of her dress hanging off her shoulder, hands pressed against the back glass, as she rode him. She didn't see me.

I stared.

Would I ever know sex like that?

Could it even be like that?

I thought people only went at it that way in books. Without sounding weird about it, Katja and Evan looked happy, ecstatic, alive and thumping, if you will. They could've made love anywhere—her place, his place, or a hotel, but they were in the car, because the car was where inspiration had struck them, and I felt a mix of shame and wonderment watching them go at it like bunnies. But also envy. Deep, burning envy to try the same with...someone.

I'd thought of Diego every night since our date, after texting him in ways that betrayed my upbringing, but damn if I didn't want what Katja and Evan had, and at some point (speaking of "dam"), mine would break.

I hurried off before she could see me and followed the smell of wood smoke and sounds of raucous laughter coming from just over the dunes. Trudging through the grassy sand-hill between mangroves, I found a bonfire in full effect and some very happy, very drunk women (and one fellow) dancing around it, whooping it up and catching each other when they stumbled. What I was seeing would've made my former self cringe. Would've made Daniel shake his head in disgust.

But I wasn't that person anymore. Not since I'd seen how open and accepting the residents of this island were. I couldn't explain it, but I felt as though I belonged here, as if maybe I'd lived here all my life and was only now remembering it. I walked up to the bonfire, pulled Sylvie's spirit board out of my bag, and asked, "Anyone up for a séance?"

fourteen

"THAT IS A BEAUTIFUL BOARD, REG!" Lily tripped up to me and lovingly ran her fingers along the edge of the Ouija board. "Where did you get it?"

"Your house."

"Mine?"

"Yes." I sighed guiltily. "I've been meaning to tell you. I found it a couple of weeks ago while cleaning your guest rooms. Actually, it was Sylvie who showed me where it was."

"*My* Sylvie?" Lily pressed a hand to her chest. "My aunt, Sylvie Collier?"

"Yes. If you're upset, I'll understand. I was going to ask you that day if I could remove it from the house, but you were so busy with taping the show."

"Oh, honey, I'm not mad at you. I'm jealous that Sylvie showed herself to you and not me, her niece, but I'm not mad." She chuckled. "Wine? Beer?"

"Wine's great. Thanks." I handed her the board, as Sam handed me wine. "She was a very easygoing spirit, comfortable with the house. And she was kind to me. Oh, thanks, Sam."

"You see her all the time?"

"I saw her once. But I know she's here a lot."

Lily's eyes glazed over. "Oh, Reg, you don't know how happy that makes me. For a while now, I wondered if I did the right thing turning her home into a bed-and-breakfast. I knew she'd considered doing the same, but I wasn't sure if she was happy with the direction I took."

"She's very happy with it. Trust me."

Lily broke into quiet tears, as Heloise pulled her in for a hug. "You can see spirits?" she asked. "Are any here now? We've been raising energy, trying to get them to come out, but I'm afraid we're not the powerful conjure mistresses that you are."

I snorted a laugh but it came out as a scoff. "Me?" Had she just called me powerful? "You're powerful. Just look what you've done to this place!" I gestured to Lily's houses down the beach. "Just look at the joy you bring others by hosting, cooking, the show, the fans, the community, the camaraderie...all of it magical."

With four sets of eyes staring at me—Heloise, Lily, Sam, and Jeanine's—my chest trembled, as old feelings of people being upset with me at hearing that their loved ones were earthbound returned.

"Us? You're amazing," Jeanine said blankly.

"Seriously, she is," Lily said. "She just doesn't know it yet."

"Why do they stick around if they're happy?" Sam asked. It was only the second time I'd ever heard his voice. He stared at me.

I sipped from my glass. "Sometimes they linger because they love a place or the people in it," I explained. "Sometimes they just want to communicate, or console you on a bad day. They don't have to be sad or lost to be here. Sometimes, they just like to visit."

"Where's Katja? She needs to hear this," Jeanine said. "She doesn't believe her Nana follows her around. Thinks it's just her conscience talking."

"Maybe it's both," Sam said.

"Maybe our spirit guides *are* our conscience, guiding us, helping us make decisions." Lily plopped next to the bonfire, still holding the board and gazing at it.

I loved everything about this. The ladies. Sam. Discussing spirituality outside of religion. For once, I had people to talk about this with. For once, I didn't feel guilty or shameful.

"Did somebody call me?" Katja strolled in from the sand dune with a bottle of wine and a glass, like nothing happened, like she hadn't just been smashing Evan's lap with her lady parts in the driver's seat a moment ago.

"Um, somebody has that glow about her," Heloise giggled.

"I was going to say," Lily said, craning her neck back to look at Katja with a big smile. "How's Evan?"

"Evan is..." Katja sighed and took a seat next to Lily. "Fucking fantastic, okay?"

The ladies and Sam all cheered.

"Yes, fine, I'll just say it. I never thought it could be this good, okay?" She gave me a pointed look. "Careful, Regina. You take a job on Skeleton Key and the next thing you know you're having two, three orgasms in a row. I don't know what it is about this place."

We all laughed and Jeanine got her butt off the sand to personally come over and clink glasses with me, then Heloise said something interesting, "The men here are a special breed. They were raised by strong women."

"That could be it." Jeanine lit up a cigarette.

"Amen to that," Katja said.

"Amen," Lily agreed.

I thought about that. Daniel had been raised by both his parents, but our family had been patriarchal in nature.

"So, Kat," Heloise said, "Regina here has offered to lead us in a little connectivity exercise with the spirit realm. You game?"

"Ooh!" Katja clapped excitedly.

"You're not gonna go all Exorcist on us, though, right?" Jeanine side-glanced me. "Because if I hear you speaking in tongues, or your head starts spinning, I'm out."

"That's not going to happen," Heloise said. "Is it?"

"I don't think so," I replied.

"You don't *think* so?" Jeanine said.

"It's never happened before. I ask for God's protection," I explained.

Heloise nodded. "Just like we do everything, babe. We call in the elements, ask Spirit for protection. Nothing that can harm us is allowed in. We control that. Should we get started? This moon party's not going to have itself."

"Let's do this." Lily shook out her hands like a boxer about to jump in the ring. "I'm nervous."

I admitted to feeling nervous, too, but with so many positively energetic people around me, I knew nothing would go wrong. My anxiety was more about showing people who I was for the very first time. "I'm really putting myself out there, just so you all know." I let out a rush of breath.

"I know how that is," Sam said.

"This is a no judgment zone, Regina. This circle here? Full of people I'd trust with my life. We should include the men sometimes," Lily said.

"No," Jeanine said.

"Why not? They're witchy too," Lily defended. "Have you ever seen Jax seal a honey jar? *Sea Witch* isn't just his boat's name, you know."

Jeanine nodded. "I don't disagree, Pulitzer. They're protectors. We're mistresses of manifestation, AKA witches." She winked at me.

Somehow, despite everything I'd ever been told, I was okay with that label. If witches healed others, helped bring them peace by connecting earthly beings with their spirit counterparts, that was just fine.

We started with a prayer led by Heloise, asking for the Goddess's protection, followed by each of them calling in different element—guardians of the east, or air; the south, fire; the west, water; and the north, earth. Lily asked for Spirit to be here to protect us, to create a shield against anything without our highest good in mind, and before long, we were all sitting tightly together, two fingers each on the spirit board, twelve fingers of six different beautiful shades of skin each.

It didn't take long for the planchette to start moving. So much energy buzzing at our fingertips, that part was natural and expected, but within a few minutes, I felt the presence of some of the same energies I'd sensed before. The firewood crackled, waves crashed against the sand, making me highly aware that the elements were working together even stronger now. I hadn't thought to invite them in when I'd done this alone.

"If anyone is here who would like to speak to us, we are open to hearing from you," I said aloud. I thought I would feel awkward voicing those words in front of others, but it was all good with this group.

Soon, the planchette began its figure eight path, slowly wandering across the wood. Nobody gasped, nobody made the sign of the cross. Just a perfectly normal action to take place while channeling spirit energy, and after a minute of it getting into a rhythm and realizing nobody here would get offended, I said, "Does anyone have a question?"

At first, nobody did. Even the witches of Skeleton Key were at a loss for words. Finally, "Would you like to tell us your name?" Sam asked.

The first letter the planchette took us to was B. After that, it was E, then L, then it wandered around for a bit before settling on I.

"Beli?" I asked.

"Grandmamá," Heloise said, chin to chest, as the planchette headed to Z. "Grandmamá Belize, thank you for being here. I love you so much. What do I say?" Her eyes leaked down her cheeks.

"Ask her if she's alone, Weezy," Katja said.

"Are you alone, Grandmamá Belize?" Heloise asked.

The planchette traveled across the board to NO. I already knew that was the case. I could see them. They materialized around us—a dark-skinned woman in a white headwrap, Sylvie in 70s-wear, Nora, Vivian's young daughter, dancing like a free spirit, and someone else staring out at sea.

"Vivian?" I asked.

I could feel the group's confusion, but the face turned toward the fire, and I saw her beautiful, sad features, same as I had in my dream. Vivian's, along with a tough-looking woman next to her I didn't know, then two more glowing forms, all of them sitting, standing, or floating idly by.

"They're all here," I said. "Not to alarm you or anything."

"Who?"

"The women of this island—your aunt—"

"Sylvie?"

"Yes."

"Josephine?" Katja asked.

"Yes, and her daughter."

Katja and Sam both gasped through smiles.

"Your grandmother has loving energy," I told Heloise whose tears dripped freely down her cheeks. "There's someone with long auburn hair holding a basket of limes."

"Annie?" Lily said. "Annie Jackson?"

"I think so. Annie, are you here with us?" I asked.

Unlike the others, I had the pleasure of seeing Annie move between Lily and Heloise, place her transparent hand on the planchette and move it to YES. Everyone squealed with glee. I didn't know Annie, but I knew she was happy with how her house had turned out and the fact that her distillery had been discovered and shared with the world.

"They're pleased with all you've done," I said, as the planchette swirled faster. It was easier this way, to speak my thoughts aloud, easier for the ghosts to send me their messages and for me to translate them. I never heard actual words, per se. I heard their intention, their messages without sentences, sometimes as emotions, sometimes as images. "But there's more work to do."

"Did she say that?" Lily asked.

The witches of long ago all looked in the same direction, down the beach, where I could see an orange glow to the south. People were flapping their arms, trying to quell flames that had erupted. Panic consumed the row of homes on the beach.

"There was a fire."

"The theater!" Katja said.

"Yes, but that wasn't the only one. Another one much later." I could hear the shouts again, the angry men—not the residents, but outsiders, men from the north who'd been hoping to purchase this land for themselves after traveling a long way on Flagler's train, men who believed promises had been made to them, only to find a thriving small resort owned by women where they'd hoped to build grand hotels. "They caused a lot of trouble."

"Who did?" Heloise asked.

"Northerners. Investors."

The spirits showed me a long trail of wooden planks on the beach, a pathway from home to home to home, being pulled apart and set on fire, the same men who'd murdered Vivian's husband. "There was a boardwalk." I kept my eyes tightly closed. I was in another world now, riding the hedge on either side of the veil.

"I knew it! Jeanine, remember I told you I always envisioned a boardwalk here?" Lily asked.

"Vivian, Annie, Josephine, they all pitched in to have it built." I saw the storm clouds in the east, the wind whipping around the palm trees. "But then there was a storm."

"The Labor Day Hurricane of 1935. That's what destroyed a lot of this island," Heloise said. "Grandmamá told me the stories."

"Yes, but the storm covered up the truth," I explained, as Vivian held her arms in the air and the sky turned to smoke. Newspaper headlines blamed the hurricane for all the damage. She wanted me to see her pain, the way she walked into the sea and took her own life. "The men were never caught."

In my chest, I could feel all these women's despondency that things never went to plan. They'd been too ahead of their time. So much work, so much investment, so many years of toiling under the sun, taking risks, and for what? For all their successes to come crashing down at the hands of the jealous.

They did it. Vivian looked straight at me.

"Who did?" I asked.

I heard her mumble something, but it wasn't clear, and I was losing energy fast, like air being let out of a large inflatable. "Guys, I'm tired," I said on the verge of getting sick again, my limit almost reached.

"Take a break," Lily said, the others agreeing.

"Say goodbye," I reminded them in case they'd never used a spirit board, and together, we swiped across the word GOODBYE. Scrambling to my feet, I walked to the water's edge and crouched there, resting my hands in the bubbling water to ground me.

Water. Mother Ocean—she'd simultaneously tried to kill me and save my life.

"Are you okay?" Katja touched my shoulder.

"Yeah. It just...gets to be a lot."

"I can imagine."

"What happened back there, Serra?" Jeanine was asking. The others were standing behind me, listening in but giving me space. Pulitzer for Lily, Serra for me—I'd gotten a Jeanine nickname.

"Is there a history of witch hunters here?" I looked up at them. Yes, witch hunters. That was what I'd heard Vivian mumble through the ether.

They all exchanged looks.

"Witch hunters? Not that I know of. Babe?" Heloise asked Jeanine, and while nobody seemed to know what I was talking about, I knew in my heart that those men who'd come to burn, murder, pillage, and destroy hadn't just come taking what they believed was theirs. They'd had a personal vendetta against each of this island's female businesswomen.

For not needing anyone but themselves.

For daring to succeed.

For dreaming up and building amazing things.

For that sin, they'd been torn down, and when they did, they set a ball into motion. "A curse," I mumbled.

"What?" Lily crouched in the sand next to me.

I looked up at all of them. "In 1935, witch hunters cursed this island. That's why all remaining businesses went down fast, and the houses haven't appreciated in value here like they have on other keys."

"I knew it!" Jeanine pressed her hands against her head. "I've been saying it for years."

"Saying what?" Lily asked.

Heloise finished for Jeanine. "That this island feels vexed, like when Atlantis Cruise Line almost bought our homes out from underneath our feet, we felt it then. If it hadn't been for you, Lily."

"Yeah, Pulitzer." Jeanine paced the sand. "I didn't know why, but I knew we had to hold onto our property as best as we could. Don't you remember? How destroyed I was when Heloise felt she had no choice but to sell?"

"I remember," Lily said.

"But you're not cursed," I said, standing, wiping my face and coming back to the present. "Not anymore. You are undoing that," I said to Lily. "All of you."

All eyes were on me.

"And you, Reg," Katja whispered.

I smiled. I hadn't done much but appreciated the recognition. "And together, you're putting Skeleton Key back on the map. Just look at it. You're literally bringing it back from the dead."

"*We* are," Lily replied.

fifteen

WHEN I AWOKE the next morning on my day off, it was to a text message from Maya asking if I could please cover her shift today. Something had "come up" with one of her friends, and she had to go help. I hadn't seen her message in time, due to my *sleeping in on my day off* and all, but apparently, it peeved her that I hadn't responded in time, since she followed up with NEVERMIND.

Sorry, I replied. *My phone was on silent.*

Normally, I would help someone out who needed it. But knowing Maya and the fact that it was Spring Break season, her emergency probably involved the friends she was staying with, a beach, and someone to mix mojitos for them, and I was not about to trade my day off so a twenty-something could party. Maybe that was mean, but I was tired of being asked for favors by people half my age who did nothing in return to help me.

No.

It felt good just thinking it. Then, I said it aloud.

"No. No, no, no."

I spent most of the day with my phone in hand, researching what I could about the island without ever getting out of bed. It was true that Skeleton Key, like most of the Upper Keys, was devastated after the Labor Day Hurricane of 1935, and one article on the Florida Historic website showed the roof of the Montero Cigar Factory blown right off. According to the website, the roof had been rebuilt, but Vivian Montero, who'd started developing many of the beachside homes into a resort, could not cope with the missing status of her husband and daughter following the hurricane; thus, ending her own life a couple of years later. She was survived by her son, Eugenio Montero, raised by a local family.

"Wow."

I sat there a long time, while the sounds of hammers, drills, and buzzsaws screeched throughout the house. Vivian Montero went through so much. Today, she wouldn't have had as many issues being a woman business-owner, but the fact that she did as much as she had back in those days was awe-inspiring. She died at the age of forty-three. At forty-three, my biggest career accomplishment had been cleaning the presidential suite at the Biltmore Hotel.

I stared at the only photo of Vivian online. Her eyes, dark and haunting, spoke volumes. Was I doing enough with my life? Vivian made me feel like I could accomplish so much more, but how did one wriggle out of a straitjacket of fear and limited opportunities?

Grabbing a pen and lighter, I headed downstairs and out front to find Mono sitting on the railing, as though waiting for me to hand him freshly made key lime pie with the limes he last gave me. "I told you, it's not that easy," I said. "Most wishes don't come true at all, you know. It's just luck."

He cocked his head, dove into the bushes, then jumped back up with an almond shaped brown fruit that had rough skin like a coconut. He handed it to me politely, for once.

"Where do you keep getting these? Are you just randomly stealing from someone's yard?" I sniffed the fruit. "Mamey, nice. Nom, nom, nom." I pretended to eat it. "Have you seen any palm fronds?"

Mono chirped inquisitively.

I wanted to try the luck spell again, the one my witchy friends did on me at Heloise's house a couple weeks back. It'd been bothering me that I hadn't fully believed that night like Jeanine said I should, and I'd learned a lot since then. In front of the bushes, near the street, I found a small, dry palm frond, located an empty, private corner of the yard away from the construction, and sat cross-legged in the sun.

Mono jumped onto my shoulder. "Let's try something. You help me, okay?" I uncapped the pen, handed Mono the cap, and wrote on the palm frond the same things I'd written that night—*for freedom from so much work, a break from physical labor, and acceptance to know that my son is at peace.*

I flicked on the lighter and was about to set one end on fire when I decided to go further. If Jeanine was right, and abundance was my birthright, then what was the harm in asking for more? Why be reserved and humble as Daniel would've said?

But what to ask for? To love again? Honestly, I wasn't sure I'd ever loved at all. As much as I wanted to feel what that was like, I wasn't sure love would be in the cards for me at this stage.

No, what I'd wanted from the very beginning, since I first saw Katja Miller walk into *House of Dolls* looking kick-ass was confidence. I wrote down, *And for the confidence to believe I'm powerful.* I tapped my cheek with the pen.

"And for some key lime and mamey treats for Mono." I wrote that down, lit the end, and waited while the dried plant caught aflame. Then, I lay it in the sandy grass, closed my eyes, and imagined it all coming true.

In the evening, I'd just come back from the Dollar Tree and dodging a few *Witch of Key Lime Lane* fans waiting in their car a safe distance from our barricades when I got a text from Diego—a selfie of him with none other than Mono on his shoulder eating from a container of ice cream.

Guess where I am?

From a hundred yards away, I could see him leaning up against the coconut palm tree outside the Montero House, phone in hand. "Where's your truck?" I called.

He whirled around. "Wow, that was fast. On the canal." He pointed to the woody area between Montero House and Mrs. Patisse.

"Your truck is on the canal?" As I got closer, I saw that Mono had stuck his head halfway inside the ice cream container. "What flavor was that, by the way?"

"Mamey," Diego said. "This was supposed to be for you, but someone made it very clear it was not."

Why was I not surprised that the little capuchin had somehow managed to manifest mamey ice cream just by wishing it? "Well, at least it wasn't key lime ice cream," I said. Because that would've been too much.

"The key lime one is over there." He pointed to the bench next to the front door where a little paper cup sat with a plastic lid on it. "I separated it, so he wouldn't eat it. He doesn't seem to get that I bring these for you, not for him, little bugger."

My jaw dropped. Mono chirped so many times in succession, it sounded like he was laughing at me.

"Want to go for a sunset cruise?"

"In your truck or scooter?" I glanced around, still not seeing any mode of transportation.

He laughed, leaned against the railing so Mono could hop off, then skipped over to get the key lime ice cream, which he handed to me. "Seriously, Reg. Have you ever seen a truck or scooter in the water?" He snorted and took me by the hand. "Come on."

What on Earth was he talking about? I didn't know, and I didn't care. I just went with Diego, despite the fact that I had a bag of groceries, because whatever Diego had planned, I knew it would be fun, and I could always make boring pasta some other time. I left the groceries on the porch, but took the ice cream.

"Why are we creeping through trees like raccoons on the run? Isn't there like, I don't know, a sidewalk or road we could use instead?"

"More adventurous this way."

I couldn't argue with that. When we finally burst through the other side of the trees, we were balancing on mangrove roots near the water which sloshed and wet my dusty, sandaled feet. "Where are we going, Diego?"

"To face our fears. To break free of monotony!"

And then, I saw.

On the edge of the water was a kayak bobbing up and down with the waves, a lone oar and a knapsack waiting inside, and just beyond, in the middle of the inlet, was a rather large fishing boat. "Is that...yours?"

"Hurry. I'm kind of illegally parked." He jumped into the kayak and held out his hand.

"I'm asking you, is that your boat?" I stepped into the kayak, using his hand for support.

"That I left unattended in the middle of a busy waterway?" he said. "Yes. Hey, I had to bring my friend ice cream. It was important. Plus, I'm kidding, it's not that busy. Come on, *niña, apúrate.*" I felt like I was in some sort of survivor game, where it was imperative that we reach the winning pile of coconuts before other contestants did.

How did Diego own that boat? And how many other things did I not know about him?

For the next few minutes, Diego rowed while we devoured a pint of ice cream, and I pondered how my life had gone from running boring errands one minute, to hopping aboard a medium-to-large fishing boat the next. I prayed we wouldn't tip over in the kayak taking us to the vessel, but I knew if we did that it was ten, maybe twelve feet deep in this area at the most.

"This is crazy," I said, watching little pipe fish in the water. "I thought you were working today."

"I was working."

"This is working? Pfft."

When he rowed, his arms looked strong. "I took a client for a spin earlier. Figured I'd get one more in before the sun went down, and I haven't stopped thinking of you, so...there you go."

My stomach crunched into a ball of nerves. Diego could not stop thinking of me? Of *me*, Regina Serra? "What kind of clients does an ice cream vendor entertain?" I asked. "A restaurant owner? Someone looking to distribute your brand?"

"Someone has a sense of business."

"Not me," I said. "I'm just guessing."

"You're not far off there, Rockefeller. I took the owner of a rather well-known fish company out for a cruise to talk about the possibility of selling my ice cream exclusively at his locations."

"Did you have to rent this boat?" I wasn't sure why I asked that. It just seemed beyond his means, but I could be wrong and from the look on his face, probably was.

"Ouch. The boat is mine, Reg." He climbed the ladder, handed me his ropey, veiny arm, and I held on while hoisting myself up. He reached down, pulled up the kayak with one fell swoop, as I did my best to stay out of his way.

"The more I think about it, the more I realize that was a stupid, offensive question," I said. "Sorry."

"No worries. I never told you I owned a boat. Then again, practically everyone who lives down here does. Anyway, it's all good. Hey..." He popped open a bench seat that doubled as a cooler, pulled out two bottles of beer, and popped them open. "Happy Day Off," he said, handing me one.

"Oh, I just had ice cream, but thanks. This is nice." It was, in fact, so nice, I felt my eyes watering up, but I forced the tears down and focused on the dazzling cotton candy colors of the western sky at dusk. "Thank you."

Diego started up the boat and moved it along the waterway, through a maze of mangroves that spilled out at the southern end of the island. There, a houseboat with all its lights on bobbed against a dock, and sitting on the front deck was a man we both recognized right away.

"My friend!" Diego waved at Sid sitting in a folding chair, enjoying his own sunset beer. I waved at Sid, too.

"Hi!" Sid took off his baseball hat in salute, dropped it back on his head, and gave us a thumb's up, as we slowly waded out to the larger body of water between the islands. Ha—who knew Sid lived on a houseboat?

Diego took us underneath Overseas Highway, around the north side of the next island where boats were gathered, their passengers all enjoying the sunset. Soon, we were back into the inlet mangrove system, surrounded by nature and silence, and I couldn't believe my luck. All my life, I'd lived in South Florida and not once had I ever been out on anybody's boat. Not once had I been given the chance to explore nature's beauty in such a relaxing way.

"Are you having fun, or is this boring?" Diego slowed the boat down to a crawl.

"Are you kidding? This is amazing!" How could he think I was bored? Had he taken other female guests out before who thought this was boring? This was so the opposite of boring! "I'm so grateful you came to get me. I'd imagined a scintillating evening of boiling pasta and reading depressing news articles all night."

He laughed, clinked his beer with mine, and piloted the boat through the tree-lined watery maze. "You can sit out front if you like."

Which I did. Totally had not thought of doing that, and part of me worried that old memories might flare up, but this ride in shallow water was so vastly different than being out in the middle of the ocean on a flimsy raft. I was okay. More than okay. The sun went down, as we watched, and from far away, we heard the cheers of twilight. Funny the way people celebrated the survival of another day.

We drifted quietly past houses—old ones that had weathered storms, the kinds up on stilts and in need of a fresh coat of paint, with rusty old rowboats bobbing by the dock, to newer, more modern, sleeker houses illuminated with fancy LED lighting on every palm tree. Both had their own kind of beauty, though the mansions were made-for-TV gorgeous.

What did people do to make this kind of money? Were they lawyers, bankers, and doctors? Had they inherited old family money? Did they work as hard as I had, or less? Or more?

One thing was for sure—they didn't think modestly about what they deserved. Nobody living in these houses thought they had more than enough or only wished for three wishes when they were asked to provide five. That much was evident. The old me under Daniel rule would've sneered at rich people, thought they were being wasteful with all that landscaping, pool lighting, and carefully constructed back-yard tiki bar islands. But the me since living here, working for Lily, admired them. Maybe they'd had a hard time like I had. Maybe they were self-made, kind people like Lily Autumn. Maybe they'd arrived to the U.S. by raft like I had, and look at them now, living the life.

Who was I to judge? I couldn't let envy make me bitter. Life was too short.

We stopped in front of one particular house that was so gorgeous with its traditional design, it reminded me of houses in Cuba of yore, the kind the rich sugar kings of the 1950s used to live in. I'd seen the family photos. Mediterranean in design with columns, archways, and beautiful Italian tile, I could just imagine men in white guayaberas strolling the grounds with cigars clenched between their teeth, striking deals for rum and sugarcane.

The boat slowed to a stop, and Diego jumped onto the edge of the boat to look at the house. After a moment of admiring it, he uncoiled the boat's rope and threw it onto the house's dock.

"What are you doing?" I asked.

"We're here."

"Where?"

"Home."

sixteen

"WHAT?" My eyeballs bulged.

He had to be kidding me.

"You're serious?"

"Of course, I am." Once he'd tied the boat to the dock, he helped me up, a good thing because I couldn't take my eyes off the waterfront mansion. Diego was taking sick pleasure in watching the cat get my tongue. He let out a chuckle. "Come on, I'll show you around."

"This is your house," I blurted.

"This is my house. Did you have something else in mind?"

Embarrassingly, I did.

"I...I don't know what I thought." I was too ashamed to tell him that I'd imagined him living in a shoddy, little apartment.

"You saw me selling ice cream and assumed I didn't make any money." He laughed. "Classic."

Nailed it.

"And now you think the worst of me," I said.

"Not at all." He led me past a row of enormous palm trees surrounded by mounds of fresh red mulch. "It's a fair assessment." Next, we walked past his elegant, rectangular pool with a walk-in shallow end and sectioned-off hot tub. Was I in a dream?

"But the wrong assessment," I said. Behind him, there were shadows moving across the walls. People here with Diego. "Is it a family house?"

He laughed again. My God, could I stop shoving my foot into my mouth? "Reg, I think you have a few pre-conceived notions about money."

"You must sell a lot of ice cream."

I loved Diego's laugh. It was low and grumbly at times, then at others, high and flute-y. Opening a French door, he stepped aside. Inside, his home was gorgeous, modern, minimalistic. The marble floors sparkled, the whole first floor had art studio lighting, and a gorgeous spiral staircase was the center of attention. On the walls were pieces of Afro-Cuban art, and the kitchen was the size of the Montero House's cigar factory room.

I tried not to ask him if we'd just broken into someone else's home.

"I don't only sell ice cream. I own a chain of eco adventure shops up and down the Keys—the place where we swam with the dolphins."

"Ocean Adventures?"

"Yep."

"But you never said anything. Why didn't you tell me when we were there?"

"Tell you what?" He slid his keys onto the kitchen counter. "That I owned the place? Why would I do that? Only a schmuck interested in showing off would brag like that. I wanted you to have a good time. And you did."

"Okay, but..." My hand clasped over my mouth. "I'm sorry to keep asking questions."

"Ask away!"

"Why, then, do you sell ice cream on the beach?"

"I love it."

"You love selling ice cream." I just wanted to make sure I was hearing him right.

"Yes. I've always made ice cream. Abuela taught me all her recipes, and I promised her before she died that I would continue making them long after she was gone."

"So, you do it to honor your grandmother?" I asked, even though I could see his grandmother, standing in the kitchen behind him, wiping her hands on a towel and nodding at me.

"I do, but besides that, I enjoy it. The eco-adventure shops are my bread and butter, but there's nothing better than making delicious desserts then watching people enjoy them." Diego made the sign for a chef's kiss.

"I guess I'm just in awe."

"Isn't there something you've always wanted to do for fun?"

"Oof." I let out a breath and stood in front of a set of hand-carved wooden figures of campesinas with baskets at their hips. "I don't have the luxury of thinking that way. You and me, we're cut from different cloths."

He frowned. "Why do you say that?"

"Because I don't have a house like this," I scoffed. "I don't have a house, period. Working thirty years with nothing to show for it."

"And you think I've always had this?"

"Whether you have or haven't, you're clearly still ahead of me in the game."

"There's no game." He walked up to me, hands in his shorts' pockets. His concerned gaze made me teary-eyed. I guess I was feeling resentful. "The only difference between you and me is that I haven't dedicated thirty years to raising a family like you have. Not a game—just circumstance."

"And you're a man. Don't forget that one. I didn't go to business school either. We couldn't even afford college."

"I didn't go to business school either," he said.

That surprised me. "You had opportunities, clearly."

"No doubt that not having kids made this easier, but my parents started small and humble in this country, same as yours. I had a business idea I thought would work well. I started small. When the first Ocean Adventures, a startup in the back of my van with two kayaks and two life vests, did well, I reinvested and bought more equipment. Then, I bought a stand outside of Islamorada Fish Company. When that did well, I opened another stand. And so on...and so on. Now I have one on every island in the chain, two in Jamaica, and two in the Bahamas."

"I guess you're a natural genius."

"*You're* a natural genius, Reg. You supported your family all those years. When you took two huge hits, you found a way to keep going when other people would've given up."

"I didn't have a choice. It was work or die."

"You *did* have a choice, and you chose to keep going. Keeping your chin up during a time of devastation is the kind of determination that makes dreams happen."

"Well, it hasn't happened."

"Yet."

"But I've decided something."

"What's that?"

"I'm going to make changes in my attitude going forward," I said.

His dark eyes lit up from within. "See, that's what I mean. People who are stuck don't think that way. Tell me, if the circumstances you think are blocking you weren't there, what would you be doing?"

I sighed. "Lily asked me the same question during my interview, and I brain-farted. I couldn't see myself in any situation other than the one I was in."

"We get in our own way with our limiting beliefs. We lie to ourselves. We tell ourselves tall tales over and over—that we cannot accomplish such-and-such because of A, we cannot achieve that because of B."

"Sounds like me a minute ago."

"Right. But I'm asking, if those limiting beliefs weren't there... Pretend you got an inheritance from a rich uncle—no need to think of money—you're taken care of for life. Now, what would you be doing?"

That was easy. "Helping people. All my life I've wanted to use my gifts."

"In what way?" He cocked his head. He wanted to know more about me? More about me he would learn.

"To help ease other people's pain."

"To become a therapist then?"

"Of sorts." Could being a professional medium be considered a therapist? "If people could receive information telling them that their loved ones made it safely to the other side..." I watched his eyes carefully. "They could find the strength to go on living."

"So, you mean..."

"Like your abuela. She's here with you. Over there, actually." I pointed at the woman smiling and waving a spatula at me. I waved back at her.

Diego's face took on a completely different tone. He looked at the vast, empty kitchen behind him, then back at me in a sort of disbelieving gaze.

"You're scared of me now, aren't you?" I said.

He stepped up to me and looked deep into my eyes. I was shaking in my stomach. "You're a brujita."

I laughed nervously, a muffled bark in my throat. "If you want to call it that. Yes." I would accept the Spanish word for witch. Why not? I'd been called that all my life.

"This is amazing. I knew there was something special about you, but I didn't know what it was. Now, it all makes sense."

"Hey. I'm the bruja, but I didn't know you owned this house, so we're even. I have to work on my skills. I've repressed them a long time now."

"Something tells me you're about to bloom."

He had no idea.

An emotional charge sizzled between us like static. I had no idea what was about to happen with him staring at me like that, like he wanted to pull me into his orbit and kiss me, let our unique energies intermingle. Again, I felt on the edge of a cliff, but in a good way.

"You know, the work you do," Diego said, "it paves the way for the bigger stuff—the passion stuff. It lights the fires of inspiration." He took my hand and rubbed my knuckles with his thumb.

I swallowed softly, my breath shallow.

"But don't forget to create the space for it. Though I was busy with work, I still made ice cream. Then, I started selling it. Just for fun. Then, I built a kitchen for it. Now, I spend half the week selling it, watching people smile, while I work the other half. Make the space, and the dream will come."

He was good at weaving beautiful words, but how would I get from A to Z? "How do I do that when I clean hotels, Diego?"

"Cleaning hotels isn't who you are. It's what you do in the meantime. You continue to do it, because you think there's no other option. You don't see a safety net. But there are other options, and you don't have to have super, extra, special skills either. I don't have any skills you don't have. Remember that."

"How do I know it's there? The safety net," I asked. It was so easy to suggest I just stop what I'd been doing for so long and pray for miracles when he lived in a place like this.

"Faith. Just like I know my grandmother is in that kitchen even though I can't see her. Don't pray for things you don't have. Imagine you already have them."

Fair enough.

"Can you help me?" I could use a little bit of Diego magic in my life. "Find the courage to jump, that is."

"Of course, I can."

We stood there, assessing each other. I had no clue what my feelings for Diego were, whether this would lead anywhere or not, or if he was passing through my life like a fishing boat on the way to Bimini. But I knew one thing—I had a friend.

"Did you say you built *another* kitchen?" I asked.

He laughed. "Yes, come on, I'll show you."

The man led me through his beautiful house, a cozy living room with a fireplace and another living room with tall ceilings and low-hanging, slowly rotating ceiling fans and lots of potted houseplants, much like Vivian's cigar factory or *Sylvie & Lily's Dead & Breakfast*. Like Diego suggested, I imagined this was my home. Big things, already mine. Hey, if a monkey could imagine limes turned to ice cream, I could do it, too.

We went down a hallway and stopped to peek into a recreation room filled with 80s-style video game machines, Skee-ball, a billiards table, and a theater-style popcorn machine. I wanted to run in and try them all.

"I'm still a little kid deep inside, Reg," he said.

"Nothing wrong with having a kid spirit," I said.

"You have to be," he said. "Or else you forget why you're doing it all for."

Lord knew Daniel never had that kidlike gene. His father always said his son had been born a forty-year-old man from Day One. There was something to be said for knowing how to have fun.

"Keeps us young and imaginative," Diego said.

And where there was imagination, there was creative energy. Hence, this house, his ice cream business, and the positivity he seemed to radiate every time I saw him.

"Here's my secret room." He stopped outside a closed steel door, looking like Willy Wonka making his guests promise not to touch anything inside his chocolate factory.

"I'm going to touch everything." I bit my smile playfully.

An eyebrow rose seductively. "I'm actually okay with that, Regina." Again with his accent. Again, his sexy gaze.

Good Lord, if I made it out of here alive against this man's charms, then he was right—anything was possible.

He opened the door.

Inside was a silvery world of stainless-steel machines, countertops, and freezers. He walked in and held out his arms. "This is my dipping cabinet. And over here are my dipper wells. Here are my scoops and dippers, thermometers, gelato pans, cold crocks." He tapped all the boxes on top of the stainless countertops.

"Wow."

"Right? And that fridge," he pointed to the corner, "has all the fresh fruits your heart could ever desire." He scooted over to the tall refrigerator and opened it. Inside were tropical fruits in every color of the rainbow.

"Where do you get them?"

"Fruit stand in Homestead. Same place Lily gets them for her kitchen. And over there is my fruit feeder, and over there is my *Extruice*."

"It's like a mad scientist's lab, but for ice cream," I said. For once, I didn't feel envious. I saw in his face and heard in his voice his kid-like enthusiasm and genuinely felt happy that he had achieved a dream, especially if he started with nothing, like me.

Diego opened a freezer, fished around, and pulled up a container. "You have to try this. Mantecado ice cream."

"What is it again?"

"It's a traditional Cuban ice cream. Kind of an egg-based vanilla flavor with a touch of nutmeg and cinnamon. Try it." He reached for a wooden paddle, scooped up a spoonful, and handed it to me.

I closed my eyes and pressed my lips around it.

They say that sometimes you feel nostalgic for places you've never been, and this was what "they" meant. All of a sudden, I saw the public square, the Spanish-Mediterranean buildings, the soldiers standing on the corners with their rifles, felt the tropical sun, the ocean breezes sweeping over the Malecón through the Havana streets, heard the old musicians playing from crumbling archways, tasted a life left behind many years ago. Most of all, I saw my parents very clearly, young and beautiful, handing me an ice cream cone. And the flavor I hadn't tasted in forty-four years?

Mantecado.

I opened my eyes, and the ghosts dissolved, just Diego there, with smiling dimples, forearms crossed over his chest, a creator who knew his worth but still hinged on my review. "Pretty darn good, huh?"

I scooped him toward me and kissed him.

seventeen

WE'D TALKED ENOUGH. There were things that needed to be said without words. Diego's mouth, warm and inviting, tasted delicious against my cold lips, a fusion I never could've imagined in a thousand dreams.

With our bodies smashed together, his hands gripped my face and hair, taking command of the kiss I'd started without knowing where the heck it was going. In a split second, I was up on the counter, knees apart, as he filled the stainless-steel space with his hips and kissed me deeper, pressing into me, wanting me in ways I knew would not be enough. It was the little things—our deep breaths, my gasps between them, his underlying groans which I knew had always been there when he looked at me, now unleashed.

We'd wanted this.

A long time.

Over a month. Ever since the day we met. And now that we were here, there was nothing to stop us. Not even my brain, which was so, so over the pain. Over the routine, bore-dom, and monotony. Over waiting for my turn. I didn't care that we awkwardly moved wheeled countertops from their spots, or that I accidentally knocked over a bin filled with sprinkles, or that we groped each other like teenagers approaching curfew. I'd never had the chance to be a teenager, to feel crazy or give into my body's innate desires before. Not like this.

How we ended up laughing our asses off as we stumbled through a side door that led onto the deck, stripped off our clothes, spilled into the pool, grinding our bodies together on the beach entry until stars exploded in the night sky—was *nothing* I would ever be able to put back together in my mind the way it actually happened. It was a fevered, technicolor dream never to be analyzed, only remembered fondly. And I knew, from the speed with which it was all happening, that I'd unblocked something.

I'd created space for the dream.

Starting with Diego.

And knew he was only the beginning.

When I arrived at work slightly late the next day, after Diego drove me by Montero House first so I could change, Maya was at *House of Dolls* to greet me at the door.

"Well, hello there." She watched me rush in, drop off my purse in a utility closet, and throw on my apron. Guests were already dining; cooks were already cooking. Maya stood there, playing with her feather duster.

I did my best to get away from her, but she followed me. "Good morning," I muttered.

"Interesting."

I stopped in the hallway and turned to her. "What is?"

153

"Nothing, you don't usually arrive *this* late."

I looked around and lowered my voice. "It's not your place to micromanage me. Got that?" I was getting tired of this little girl.

Maya bristled. "All I said was 'interesting.'"

"Like I said, I don't need another boss, especially one who isn't here for the reason she says she is. I have one boss, and that's Lily."

A slow smile unfurled on her lips. "Ahh. So, you *did* listen to my conversation that day."

"Anyone would have. You were talking loud enough for the roosters in Key West to hear you. But don't worry, I don't want a spot on TV. I'm here to clean and be unseen. I'm not your competition." I started walking away.

"Actually, you are."

I paused, watching her wave her duster over a mirror.

"Lily is an older woman. Katja's an older woman." She looked me up and down, trying to make me feel irrelevant, but nope. "You're an older woman. It just makes sense that you're next."

"Trust me, I don't have the charisma to be a show host. You, on the other hand...full of charm. The perfect choice." I smiled.

She pressed a manicured hand to her chest. "Aww, thank you." I was not about to explain that I was being facetious. "Did you know Lily flew out last night to go see her kids?"

"No, I didn't."

"Oh. I thought maybe that was why you didn't sleep at home last night."

I stopped at the bottom of the stairs, hand on the bannister. "First of all, it's none of your business where I sleep. I'm twice your age. Okay?" I was not having it. She was lucky I was in a good mood. "And second of all, what Lily does is not my business. I do my job well regardless of whether or not she's watching me."

"Does that include stealing from her house?"

"Excuse me?"

"You took a Ouija board from the guest bedroom. Everyone saw you walking with it under your shirt." She chuckled.

"Who's everyone?"

"Serge."

"The security guard? That's one person."

She ignored me. "Even with your boyish body, he could still see it." She may as well have told me I was shaped like a rectangle, the better to hide a Ouija board with.

"Why would he tell *you*?" I drilled a look into her. "Serge doesn't work for you. He works for Lily."

Her tongue tucked into the corner of her mouth. I'd seen the way she befriended the guard. Good way to get special favors. I'd seen it all before.

I smiled. "I love how every time you open your mouth, you incriminate yourself." I'd never been one to fight, but that didn't mean I wouldn't unleash hell in my own special way.

This could've gone any number of ways. At the moment, memories of Daniel's mother's telenovelas where the characters strike out into catfights came to mind. But I was not dramatic, nor an actress, and I understood Maya's need to tear me down—she believed I was a threat.

Knowing this brought a smile to my cheeks, which already hurt from all the smiling I did last night after sampling Diego-flavored ice cream. I'd never been a threat to anyone before. Being a threat meant having power, and having power was also on my list of never-before-experienced-stuff. These last twenty-four hours were turning out to be delightful, indeed.

"Better get back to work," I said, pointing at the restroom behind her. "Toilets don't clean themselves. Oh, and just so you know, I won't be sleeping at 'home' again tonight either. I'll be busy."

I snorted a laugh.

It was late after an intense bed-wrestling session with Diego. Possibly two or three in the morning. All the lights on in his room. We were talking about the island, the Montero House, and the fact that many residents knew the house was haunted. I was curled up next to his warm side, listening to him talk, but too many thoughts churned in my mind—the way Maya had spoken to me like *una malcriada,* the energy I got from her as though she were trying to find dirt on me, and the fact that she hadn't responded the way I'd hoped when I told her I wouldn't be sleeping at Montero House tonight.

Instead of acting surprised, she'd shrugged, seemed satisfied, then totally dropped the subject.

"Did you know my great-grandfather worked there?" Diego said through a yawn.

I sat up. "At Montero House?"

"Yep, name was Manolo Joyas. Lots of people worked there. I'm sure, if you wanted to, you could trace at least twenty-five percent of the longtime residents of this area back to someone who worked on Skeleton Key."

"What did he do at Montero House?" I asked.

"He was one of their *lectores*, the guys that would read aloud to the workers to keep them entertained. It's an old practice."

My eyes lit up. "No way! I saw him."

"You saw my great-grandfather?"

"It might've been him. I saw a well-dressed man come into the factory and start reading from a newspaper in a theatrical voice."

"Sounds devilishly handsome. Had to be my great-grandfather." Diego laughed, shot out of bed, and searched through his closet. From the upper shelf, he brought down a large, withered box and set it on the bed. "I even have some of his books and newspapers," he said, pulling stacks of folded old papers. "The dude kept everything he ever read."

He handed me one with a headline about the economic depression in the United States. Then another one about the Labor Day hurricane. Then, another one: *Béisbol en Cuba gana popularidad!* Cuban baseball gains popularity.

"This is the same paper he read from!" Just holding the paper in my hand, I felt the vibrations of the Montero's cigar factory and the man who'd read there. I could see the chair in which he'd sat, the potted palms, the checkerboard floor.

It was almost as if the paper and the house were still connected. I even saw it now, empty and losing its identity with the past with every renovation they completed. Soon its energy would be gone.

"Are you okay?" Diego caressed my hair.

"I feel like I have to go."

"Now? It's so late."

"I'm sorry. Can you drop me off?"

"Of course. I'll get my shoes on."

"And some clothes." I winked at him.

He grabbed a pair of shorts and pointed them at me. "Hey, these are the tropics. Clothing optional."

I got dressed, too, and within a few minutes, we were driving back down Overseas Highway, the windows open, salty air whipping my hair. The house was calling me back, I had no idea why. When we arrived on Mango Road, I said, "Drop me off here."

"I'd feel more comfortable if you let me—"

"Here is fine," I insisted. I knew there was a chance of being seen by Serge or Rick, whichever security guard was on duty, and since Serge was buddies with Maya, I didn't want to be noticed. "I'll call you tomorrow."

Hopping out of his truck, I took the path through the mangrove trees, cutting behind homes, sneaking through the vegetation like a heron in search of breakfast. When I reached the path where Diego had tied his kayak, I made a left and snuck all the way to Montero House. Seeing it sitting alone and forlorn in the darkness made me sad, but even from a distance, I could tell something stirred within.

Voices.

But not ghosts.

I crept closer to the front porch, using the trees' shadows to my advantage. Halfway down the street, I could see the silhouette of Serge pacing up and down in the moonlight, like keeping watch. Through an open window, I thought I heard a woman's voice.

Not Vivian.

Not Nora.

There were other voices as well, along with crossed streams of flashlight through the windows. People unauthorized by Lily Autumn were here. Could Maya have finally decided to sleep here one night, since I said I wouldn't be here? Friends? Party? Sleepover? Why on Earth would she want to host anything here when there was nothing but dust and construction?

I pulled open the side door to the kitchen and snuck in, crouching low to the ground. From the sounds of it, they were gathered in the cigar rolling room, the one getting its new floors installed, about four or five people altogether, both men and women's voices. Creeping to the edge of the counter, I sat in the darkness listening. I supposed I could just walk in and declare I was home, but these didn't sound like friends of Maya's. I wasn't even sure it was her.

I strained my hearing to catch words and phrases.

"Why don't we..."

"...Estes Method in this room."

"Or, EMF detector in the other two...REMpod in the kitchen?"

"Yes, that way, we cover all bases of the downstairs, then we can use the Ouija board upstairs for the second half of the night."

I didn't recognize the man who spoke. Never heard him before in my life. Who gave him permission to be on the premises? And which Ouija board did he plan on using? Better not be Sylvie's.

"Does that give you enough time?" A woman's voice echoed through the house, though I couldn't place anybody's. "You have to be out of here by 5 AM the latest.

The cleaning lady who lives here does her Walk of Shame around sunrise. I need everyone gone by then."

Maya?

I held my breath, as a fire sparked inside of me. Walk of Shame? "The Cleaning Lady?" What right did a cleaning lady have calling me a cleaning lady? I wanted to rush out there and blow the whistle, tell maybe-Maya and her little ghosthunting friends that, not only was the party over, but Lily Autumn would be finding out about it as well. Extra points deducted for using a sacred item that had belonged to Sylvie Collier without her permission.

But there was no way to know for sure that it was Maya, and suddenly, something whizzed through the darkness and landed on my shoulder, tiny little nails grasping my collarbone and hair at the same time. My mouth opened to shriek but I clasped my hand over my maw and cut the scream short.

"Did you hear that?" another female voice said.

Mono chirped loudly. I clamped my hand over his little face to quiet him. He bit my finger—*son of a bitch*—and I bit my tongue to keep from crying out. He scuttled off my shoulder, just as footsteps shuffled hurriedly in the next room. They were coming to see what had made the noise.

"It sounded like a woman crying."

"I heard a child's voice."

If I didn't want to be caught crouching in the kitchen in my own place of work, I had to move quickly. Crawl back out the side door, make my presence known loudly and proudly, or... I watched with cat eyes adjusting to darkness as Mono opened a kitchen cabinet door near the floor, one usually filled with pots, now empty, and disappeared inside.

Yeah?

Well, this petite "boy's body" could do the same. I went in after him, folding up my frame inside the cabinet, emptied and readied for demolition, and noticed that the capuchin monkey was no longer with me. *Wait a minute.* There wasn't much room inside. I would know—I was folded up like a pretzel. As I heard cautious footsteps coming into the kitchen, I lit up my phone screen and noticed the back of the cabinet had a panel—a very old wooden sliding panel that blended in with the cabinetry.

Mono had disappeared.

Into a secret room.

So, that's where the little shit hides.

And before some ghosthunters who weren't even allowed to be here could catch me hiding in my own "home," I slipped into the space, too, and gently closed the sliding panel behind me.

eighteen

I SAT IN ABSOLUTE SILENCE, listening to my
own heart beating, willing it to quiet down so I could hear
better. The absurdity of what I was doing crossed my mind.
From inside this crawl space beneath the house, I couldn't
hear what the kids were up to on the floor above, couldn't
tell them to leave either. I was hiding, as if *I* were the one
who'd broken in.

Next to me, fiddling with something on the sandy, grassy
ground on which Montero House was built, was Mono. I lit
up my phone screen to see him better and saw him sticking
his head inside a discarded paper cup with *The Sweet Spot*
printed on it. There weren't just two or three, there were at
least two dozen scattered everywhere. He must've been
stealing from garbage cans or wherever guests were
throwing them away after they were done.

Also in the crawl space were an inordinate number of
cobwebs, tall tufts of beach grass, copper pipes, and other
underbelly parts to a house. Beyond the two-foot perimeter

of phone screen light surrounding me was nothing but more musty darkness.

"Really? You have a secret lair where you collect empty cups?" I whispered. "I know it's good, but isn't that a bit desperate?" Said the woman hiding underneath a mansion with a monkey. "Well, it's a good hiding spot. I'll give you that."

While I appreciated having the space to hide and think about my next move, I would not stay here another minute. I would go up there and give the intruders a piece of my mind. And if one of them *was* Maya, no wonder she'd stared at me funny when I told her I wouldn't be sleeping here tonight. How long had she been waiting for this opportunity to let in her ghost hunting friends? Had they paid off Serge for the access while Lily was out of town?

Something else occurred to me. These kids had come for a thrill or two at a haunted house. Why not give them more than they bargained for?

"Watch and learn," I said to Mono.

He chirped.

Listening intently, I waited until there was a good lull in their conversation before reaching a few inches above my head and counting down in a whisper, "Three...two..." I pounded on the ceiling with all my might.

Suddenly, squeals and screams echoed above us, and footsteps scattered in all directions. Through the floorboards, I heard them shouting and giving each other orders over where to point the camera to capture evidence of the haunting. I couldn't help it and laughed quietly into my hands.

"It's coming from over here! Bring the camera! Bring it here!" one of the men shouted.

"You do it. I'm leaving," someone said.

"Guys, I'm out," I heard the one that might have been Maya say. "Stay if you want."

Poor ghost hunters, unable to handle a little paranormal activity. If they only knew what the real stuff was like. I pounded again and again, enough times to make the investigation crew regret their visit. Indeed, the Montero House was haunted.

Not the way you might think, though.

Footsteps pounded all over the floor, scattering like ants, voices fading away. When it seemed like they had all fled outside, I waited. I wouldn't come out and confront them after all, or they would realize the "poltergeist" wasn't real. I waited about fifteen minutes while car engines turned on and the sounds of cars driving away told me the coast was clear.

I waited a few minutes more, in case they came back with Serge or someone new. Mono decided he felt safer in my lap. I scratched his head. "I'm under a house with a monkey," I muttered, turning it into a little tune to keep myself company. "Under a house with a monkey...scaring kids off... surrounded by paper cups. What is my life?"

My life, as fact would have it, had been livelier in the last several days than it'd ever been in forty-seven years, and thinking of Diego in this empty, quiet space made me smile.

Finally, I crawled back toward the hidden sliding door of the cabinet, my knees scratched up and my skin slick with sweat.

Quietly, I slid the door aside, pushed the cabinet open

with my fingertips and poked my head out. I listened for sounds, but when it was clear that they'd all left, I climbed out and stood in the kitchen, straightening my old hag's back, thanking my limberness, and breathing in deep lungs full of air.

"That was crazy," I whispered. "Thanks for showing me that space, Mono. Best prank ever, am I right? Mono?" The little guy had stayed inside the crawl space. I patted my pocket, considering texting Diego to tell him about the weirdest hour I'd ever had when I realized I left the phone inside the crawl space. "Ugh."

Fine, but there was no reason I had to crawl around in the dark anymore. The kids had left. I flicked on the kitchen switch, grateful for the grounding fluorescent light of reality and opened the cabinet again. With my head inside and my butt sticking up in the air, I slid open the secret doorway.

My phone lay in the sand, the flashlight still on and facing up, creating concentric circles in the wood above it. Mono sat next to it, gnawing on a mango seed pod.

"Pstt...hand me my phone. Please?" I asked him. When he looked up from his seed pod, I pointed to the phone. "That. Pass it to me?"

Adorably, he understood, grabbed the phone and skittered over to give it to me with a chirp.

"Thank you. What a kind little monkey you are! Now, let's go. You shouldn't be hanging out in a place like this."

Except he didn't hand it to me. He backed up some more and sat on his haunches, holding my phone.

"Nooo, bring it here," I said.

He backed up a few more inches.

"Mono? I said, bring it here." I held out my hand.

He backed up again, smiled with gums exposed. Little shit. He was going to make me climb back in, wasn't he? "I'll give you all the ice cream you want," I bartered with him. "I'll hook you up. I know a guy."

But Mono was having too much fun playing his control game. He skittered back again and sat in the far recesses of the crawl space, thoroughly entertained by my phone. With the flashlight still on, he moved it around and around enjoying the way the ceiling lit up as if by searchlights.

"Don't make me come after you. If I have to crawl back in there, you are not going to be a happy monkey. You hear me? I'm going to start counting."

He wouldn't budge.

"Alright. Here I go. Hand me that phone in one...two...two and a half..."

He couldn't care less about my threats. He flipped the phone over in his hands, scuttled back another few inches to escape my wrath, then held the phone still. For the moment he did, the flashlight shone on something behind him. I shifted my weight to the side, so the fluorescent light of the kitchen behind me could squeeze around my shoulders and into the darkness.

That was when I saw them—feet.

And they'd been dead a long time.

nineteen

THE AIR TURNED MUGGY.

My mouth filled with hot saliva.

I stared wide-eyed at the crusty, skeletal feet—two sets of them, intertwined—for as long as I could until tunnel vision got the best of me, then I was gone, drowning, sinking again.

Down, down...

The radial sunburst high above the surface, the only source of light, got smaller and smaller. It was love and life itself, out of my reach. Alone. So alone for so long. It could've been a minute since I'd had someone to talk to. It could've been years. All I knew was that I was waiting again, for someone to find me, rescue me.

Drowning... Drowning...

Into the quiet, watery depths, forever and ever. But this was a dream, wasn't it? Not a life sentence.

I wasn't dead like the dried-out husks of long-ago humans hidden in the crawl space. How long did I have to wait here until someone found me? I could easily be here a hundred years or more before someone, way off in the future, discovered me sinking. Unless I moved. Unless I stopped waiting for rescue and rescued myself. Unless I tried to swim. This was my life, and these visions weren't set in concrete. They were as fluid as the ocean, and I could mold them anyway I wanted.

I was thinking of the malleable nature of just this, how I had more control than I thought, that I wasn't a victim needing rescue anymore when suddenly, Vivian was there. With me, suspended in the ocean, a black and white dress billowing around her, beautiful dark hair like a Medusa halo.

Have you seen them? Have you seen my husband and daughter?

I have! I cried without words. For once, I could help her find the answers she sought. *They're under the house. They've been under the house this whole time! They were murdered, their bodies hidden! I saw them!*

Her eyes closed a moment, as she absorbed my words like medicine for her pain. She'd always known in her heart they'd been murdered, but she'd never received confirmation. Nobody but those responsible for their deaths could know for sure, and they'd been dead a long time now, their own spirits probably in a world of hurt for the troubles they'd caused while on Earth.

Vivian smiled, as tiny bubbles flitted and danced around her. She was disappearing, getting lighter, wispier, both in mass and in vibration, as her despair subsided. Her tears filled the ocean, salty jewels of anguish mixing with the sea until they were completely absorbed. I envied her, being able to shed the heartache.

Thank you, she said.

A smile formed on her lips, as though she'd always known but needed to hear it from someone else, needed validation of her worst nightmares come true.

Maybe you can find them? I suggested to her. *If you move into the light...* I looked above at the starburst growing brighter, whiter, its brilliance taking up more of the wide blue sky. *If you move into the light, I'm sure you'll see them. Why don't you try?*

Yes, she said. *There's nothing left for me here.*

Good. I wanted so much to help her past this. I reached out for her hands. It was sad that there was nothing left for her on Earth, just like one day, there would be nothing left for me. We were nothing but blips of time, temporary cells of breath and tissue in a vast cosmos made of light. Her hands felt like nothing. She was made of ether and starlight.

The business, the house, the money...meant so much to us, but without anyone to share it...

I gave her a sad, understanding smile. Without anyone to share it all, it meant nothing, and where she was going, she couldn't take it with her.

Take it for yourself.

She said this, as if I could just take a house that now belonged to someone else decades into the future. Vivian Montero had no clue what century I was living in, no idea that it wasn't the 1930s anymore, that several families had lived in her home since she departed, no idea her home now belonged to someone else.

And the notes in the fireplace.

Have them.

Notes? As in, music? The gramophone I'd seen?

With that, she began a dance, a slow swirling vortex

upwards through the water, higher, a slowly spinning torpedo, her dress twirling around her, as though the sun itself were drawing her towards it, like moths to a flame. Except it wasn't the sun—it was the light of source energy, the intelligence that held us all together. Some called it Heaven. Some called it God. I called it Love. Vivian called it Home.

And then, my eyes opened.

And it was morning.

And my throat felt clogged with dust. And my tongue was glued to the ceiling of my mouth.

How long had I been asleep? And why was I stuck inside a wooden box with my legs sticking into...the kitchen? It took me a moment to place myself, but when I heard a chirping behind me and felt a little mammal shift his body on my butt, I remembered. Suddenly, it all came rushing back to me, where I'd been. A cabinet. Mono. My phone. Feet—there were dead feet, dead people inside the crawl space.

I'd felt so sick, I'd passed out.

Wait—feet?

I could see them now clearly with the morning sun's rays filtering in through the wooden junctures of the house's underbelly. What used to be a white dress, now yellowed and brown, sank into the sand. Next to it was a suit of faded blue that rose and fell in line with the wavy sand. I couldn't see much else from this angle.

I scrambled out of the cabinet faster than I could blink and rubbed the crick in my neck. Mono watched me with a very concerned expression.

"I'm okay. I think..." My head hurt. My heart hurt.

The monkey handed me my phone.

Smirking, I took it. "Thanks," and looked at the time. 7:34 AM. I was way late for work, but I wouldn't be going to work right now, and if I got fired for that, so be it. I had to make a few phone calls first. Out by the street. Not in here. I didn't care how accustomed to death I was in the form of ghosts, I didn't want to be near dead bodies, no matter how long they'd been there.

I bolted outside and considered calling Andreas. Then, I realized I'd have too much to explain and decided on calling Diego instead. Sure, I could've called Lily, Katja, or any of the *Dead & Breakfast* folks, but I needed an unbiased, untethered opinion, and Diego was my only real friend here.

He answered on the first ring. "There you are. I've been texting you all morning. Usually you're up by now."

"There's dead people."

"I'm sorry?" I could hear the wind whipping around him.

"They've been dead a long time, but I just found them. Can you come over and help me?" For a moment, I doubted my own memory. What if Diego got here, stuck his head in the crawl space, and didn't see anything?

Could I trust my own experiences? Was I going insane?

"I have a meeting in twenty minutes with a hotel owner," he said.

"Don't worry about it," I said. "I can deal with it."

"No. I'll be right there. Give me fifteen minutes." He hung up, as I waited on the stoop of the house. Any minute now, construction workers would arrive, disrupting the quiet and solitude of this early spring morning.

I had to call the police and report the bodies. I had to call Lily. I had to call Andreas and let him know at some point, because surely, this would be on the news, and he might see it and worry. But for now, I enjoyed the quietude of the beach town, Mrs. Patisse coming out of the house to pick up the newspaper from her lawn. I waved at her. She waved at me. I tried not to break down from the simplicity of it.

Why was it I encountered death everywhere, spoke with spirits every day, but couldn't speak with my own son? Why wouldn't Pablito visit me in my dreams?

"You can come to me, you know. Like everyone else does." I told the empty air around me. I closed my eyes and imagined him here, walking up the walk, bringing me coffee before he left for work—lots of cream and sugar, a little touch of cinnamon.

"Thank you, *hijo*," I said, as if the coffee were in my hands. "I miss you so much."

When a car I'd never seen before pulled up, and a superbly handsome devil I barely recognized stepped out wearing slacks, a guayabera, a platinum watch, and a hat like he was going to play dominoes with old men in the park, I wasn't sure who I was looking at. "Hey."

"I barely didn't recognize you."

He jangled the keys of his...BMW? And took off his hat. "Told you, I was on my way to a meeting."

"You didn't have to cancel it, but thank you for coming. Do you have a flashlight?"

He reached into the glove compartment, then stepped out of the car holding a Maglite. "I postponed. It's okay. I want to help. What's going on?" He hopped over and leaned in for a quick hug, but even lovely-smelling Diego could not dissolve my jangled nerves. "Geez, Reg, you're shaking."

"Am I? I'm not sure what I've seen. I need someone to double-check for me. You're going to get those nice clothes dirty." I said, leading him into the house and then the kitchen. I opened the last bottom cabinet, slid open the secret door, then gestured.

"Then I'll change clothes afterwards. No big deal." Diego got on his knees and stomach and tried wedging his much bigger body as far as he could into the crawl space, stopping at just his shoulders. "What am I looking for?" he shouted, his voice muffled.

"All the way in the back. You don't see something odd?" I waited what felt like a long time. My worst fear was that I was going crazy, that I'd called him over to locate something I'd only seen in my imagination or third eye. After all, it had been in the wee hours of the morning.

"Well?"

One inch at a time, he wriggled his way back out, switched off the flashlight, and sat on the floor out of breath with his hands perched on his knees. "That's a lot of *Sweet Spot* cups in there."

"Diego! Did you see anything else?"

"I hate to tell you this..."

Ugh. So, I did imagine it. I covered my face.

"But there's two crispy skeletons back there."

"Right?" I spun in a circle and pulled out my phone to call the police. "I knew it. Knew it!"

"Who are they?"

"I think they're your great-grandfather's employer and daughter. They went missing during a hurricane way back in the 1930s. Authorities told Vivian Montero that they were probably killed during the storm, but she never found them."

"Maybe the storm surge pushed them under the house?" he suggested.

I shrugged. "I don't know. I don't think so." Why would they both be there together?

"Your sources tell you otherwise?" He raised an eyebrow.

I gave him a pointed look, making sure he wasn't making a joke. If he couldn't accept me for who I was and believe me, we would never, ever have a chance together. I'd already lived that life once. No traces of sarcasm on his face. "Yes," I said clearly.

"Damn, woman. You should be working as a psychic detective."

I tried to smile. No wonder this house had held onto negative energy. No objects were more cursed than murdered bodies themselves, sitting there all this time. They needed to be extracted and given a proper burial, so Nora and Vivian could rest in peace.

By the time the police arrived, I'd called Lily in New York, and she'd sent Jax, Sid, Heloise, and Jeanine to the house on her behalf. Lily said she would be getting on a plane back to the Keys tonight. Heloise kept her arm around my shoulder, a gesture I deeply appreciated. Once I'd filed a report and the neighbors and onlookers at the end of the barricaded road went back to their lives, Diego left to his meeting, and I headed upstairs to get something important while they were busy extracting the bodies.

While the workers carefully put the two corpses on cloth stretchers, I nervously stood on the sidewalk, bauble in hand, waiting for the right moment, and when they finally walked past me toward their truck, I tucked Ramón Montero's cigar pick ornament—the bauble from the beach —back into his pocket.

"God be with you," I murmured.

Cursed object be gone.

At work, even Maya knew better than to talk to me. I would never be the same again, and for the next several days, the house was quiet. No ghosts. No dreams. No offerings of flowers. No disturbances. No nightmares. Like a heavy veil lifted, the sadness had gone. The ghosts of the Montero House had moved on.

On the night before my next day off, I opened the bottom drawer of my nightstand, stared at Pablito's bloody shirt, then slept with it under my pillow for the last time. Time for me to move on, too.

twenty

ANOTHER FULL MOON, another moon party.

I arrived at the beach as a guest for the third time to find a dinner table set up underneath a small canopy—lilies in vases, pale green runners, lilac chargers, and white fine china. Beautiful hand-painted Easter eggs adorned the table, and each plate had a resin bunny sitting in the middle of it.

"Is it Easter? I don't even know what day it is anymore," I said, marveling at all the candles, twinkling lights, and dinner magic these ladies had conjured up.

"Worm Moon," Jeanine muttered, a cigarette clenched between her teeth. "Or Lenten Moon, last one of winter."

Heloise popped a shrimp in her mouth and talked with her mouth half-full. "Time for renewal, sowing new seeds, making plenty of space for growth. So mote it be."

"So mote it be," Lily said.

"Amen. Oh, here." I handed Lily a box of cookies from the Publix bakery. "Sorry, I didn't get the baking gene like you ladies did."

"Reggie..." Lily accepted the box and lay a hand on my shoulder. "We all have our talents. Mine's cooking, Heloise's is baking, Sam and Katja's is dollmaking, Jeanine's is being a pain in the ass..."

"Hey!"

"And yours is solving century-old mysteries. Thank you, for the cookies and for the publicity on my new house."

"That's right! New house, new *Dead & Breakfast*, coming right up," Heloise cheered, welcoming me to sit down at the head of the table. "To Regina!"

"To Regina!" Lily handed me a glass of wine.

"To Regina," Katja and Sam said, toasting to me.

"To Skeleton Key's first occult detective." Jeanine held her glass high in the air, but we all just looked at her like she'd spoken some other language.

"First what?" I laughed.

"What the frick are you talking about?" Heloise looked at her wife. "Girl, you high already?"

"An occult detective," Jeanine said, waving her cigarette around. "You know, Mulder and Scully, Harry Dresden, the Ghostbusters, Scooby-Doo. People who help solve mysteries —supernatural ones."

"Ohhh," we all groaned.

"I hate to tell you, though," I said. "But Montero House isn't haunted anymore. At least not that I've seen or felt. So, I don't know how much publicity you'll get."

"Shh, don't tell anybody that," Lily chuckled. "It's all part of the allure, the guest experience. Besides, you never know, there could be more."

"True," I said. "So, you're definitely converting it to

another guest house?" I asked, digging into the wonderful appetizers on the table—shrimp, deviled eggs, some delicious honey-glazed ham canapés.

"Not sure. We have to see how Season 2 performs. Could be another eight months to a year before we know."

I imagined Maya dying to be a fly at this party, just to hear Lily mull the idea of another season over with her friends. I couldn't imagine her working at *House of Dolls* another eight to twelve months just to get on Lily's good list.

Once I reported the bodies last week, Lily found out there'd been interlopers at the house, because I had to explain why I'd been hiding in the crawl space. What she didn't know, however, was that Maya may have been among them, and I hadn't brought it up because I couldn't be sure. However, seeing how much effort my witches had put into dinner, I decided I'd broach the subject tomorrow.

After dinner, we sat around the fire, drinking, chatting, and staring up at the moon, basking in her bright light of fullest possibility. The night was warmer than it'd been in the last two months since I'd been here, a sure sign of spring, and the ocean was the calmest I'd ever seen it.

"I brought something else with me tonight," I confessed, once I'd finished my second glass of wine.

"Oh? What's that?" Katja tossed dry seagrass into the fire to watch it burn.

I reached back for my purse sitting on the sand and pulled out the plastic bag. Then, taking a deep breath, I extracted Pablito's blood-soaked Captain America shirt.

"Do we even want to know what that is?" Jeanine's cigarette bobbed up and down between her teeth.

They leaned in to see what I had. "It's my son's. He was wearing it the night of the accident."

Someone gasped.

I kept my eyes on the shirt. "I've kept it too long. I need your help letting it go."

Heloise swept into my side, as she always did. "Of course, you do, honey. No wonder you feel stuck. You shouldn't have that. You know that."

"I know."

"If I'd have known, I would've made you get rid of it sooner," Lily said.

My eyes filled with hot tears. "But it was the last thing he wore while he was alive. It even smells like him." I choked up and felt the familiar wave of pain seizing my body. Rather than fighting it, I welcomed it, acknowledged it. "How am I supposed to..."

The words got stuck.

"Shh, shh..." They surrounded me. "Okay, you're okay..."

I *would* be okay—I knew that deep in my heart—but first I needed to acknowledge how much it hurt that my son might never visit me, that somehow I'd have to live the rest of my life without his sweet ways. I needed to acknowledge lots of other things, too.

"Dear Universe, please help our friend Regina to know that her son is always with her," Lily prayed over me. "Please ease her pain and help her to know that the best way to honor her son's memory is by living the most amazing life she can, in his name."

"As above, so below," Jeanine said.

"I wish that were true," I muttered.

"What, honey?" Heloise said.

I lifted my face, cheeks stained with tears. "I said I wish that were true, that he is always with me. I call to him, I talk to him, I ask him to come to me. I want to know that he is with me, but I never hear from him. I see all of your beautiful loved ones, I see ghosts in every house I visit, but I don't see mine."

"Oh, honey," Heloise purred.

"Let's take care of that," Jeanine said. "Right now. Come over here, Serra. Come on."

Holding Pablito's shirt, I got up and trudged through the sand.

"This," she said, reaching out and holding it up at eye level, "is not your son. It's just a shirt." She looked at the tag. "Made in China. Okay? Your son is in your heart. He's in your mind, he's in the world around you. He's in your smile when you look in the mirror."

"Babe, she knows that," Heloise whispered, trying to rein her wife in, but I didn't mind. She was right, and I needed to hear it.

"If you're going to keep a charged object, keep the good ones," Jeanine said. "His baby blanket, his teddy bear, any gift or piece of art he made as a child. Those bring joy and happiness. Nothing wrong with keeping a few things to remind you of that sweet boy."

I couldn't speak.

My throat was clogged with heartbreak.

"But this?" She shook the shirt. "This is filled with pain. It's time for you to release all that doesn't serve you and keep what does. Ask Katja, she'll tell you."

Katja nodded. "SpongeBob voodoo doll, anyone?"

Ah, so she'd burned the cursed object I'd first seen in her memory. No wonder she was so alarmed when I dredged it back up from the past. "I know." I caught my breath and wiped my eyes. "That's why I brought it. I just wanted you all to do it with me."

"Then, let's do it." Jeanine raised a triumphant fist in the air. "They don't call us the Skeleton Key Witches for nothing!"

"They don't call us that, babe," Heloise said.

"They most certainly will one day!" Jeanine declared.

Together, we gathered around the shirt, as I struggled with words. "*Mi amor,* this only reminds me of the way you went out, not the way you came in, nor the life you lived. I don't want to remember the pain more than the happiness, so from now on, I'll only keep the happy keepsakes. I know you'll agree."

I kept my son in my mind's eye, knowing he would want me to get rid of it.

"It doesn't mean I don't love you," I sniffed. "Or that I'm letting go of you. You are always in my heart."

Lily ran off to our bags of stuff and came back with a Sharpie. "These come in handy," she said, handing it to me. "Write words on that shirt. Feel free to add anything else that you want to let go of."

"Oh, God." So. Much. Stuff. It would take me the whole night to think of them. But I did my best to focus on the big ones. I wrote:

Resentment, thinking of my upbringing, the life Daniel had wanted for us, and my current financial situation.

Anger, thinking of my son's death.

Sadness, thinking of my son's death again.

Pain, thinking of the shitty hand life had dealt me.

But had it really? Because I had things other people didn't have. I'd been taken care of by another family after mine perished. I'd been kept safe from the harm a government wanted to inflict on me. I had freedom in this country. I had rights. I had the opportunity to turn things around if I really wanted to; it would just take some creativity and a stroke of luck.

That was enough for now. I read each one aloud, adding any extra thoughts, and listened as they repeated each one aloud with me. It felt good to have backup, to know I had friends, that I didn't have to do this alone. By the end, I was ready to say goodbye to the shirt.

Like Jeanine said, it was just a shirt.

We tossed it into the fire, danced the rest of the night, as I allowed myself to feel a hundred times lighter than I ever had before, and said goodbye to Pablito...again.

I was in the ocean, except this time, I wasn't drowning. I wasn't swimming either. I just sank deeper and deeper, no burning sensation in my lungs, no panicking, no feeling on the verge of dying. Instead, I hovered peacefully suspended in midwater, similar to how Vivian had floated when she'd visited me last time.

I was dreaming again, and I knew it. I also knew I could bend the dreamscape, too, shape it, make it twist to my will. I was in total control, doing somersaults in the water. High above was the sunburst in the wide blue sky, and floating on the water, the darkened silhouette of a boat. I could go to the boat if I wanted to, or I could stay here.

Except "here" was so lonely, in the middle of the ocean with nothing but particles of plankton floating around. Nobody to talk to, nobody to laugh with. No fires to dance around. No bodies to kiss in a fevered sweat. No ghosts to help, no earthly worries with which to occupy my time. It wasn't horrible, but it wasn't great either. It was time for me to leave the ocean behind for good.

I awoke in a sweat with the moonlight spilling into my room and felt the ocean's pull calling to me outside like a lullaby in the night. Tearing off my drenched T-shirt, I opened the shutters and gazed outside, still half asleep. The moon glowed over the ocean—the beautiful waters of the Atlantic who could hurt or heal, depending on how you saw them.

Though it was four in the morning, I headed downstairs through the dusty, cavernous body of the first floor with its wooden beams, sheets of drywall, new ceiling fans, and cut pieces of molding everywhere. I ran my hand along the fireplace for good measure. Opening the new French doors, still with their brand-new pieces of plastic sheeting on the glass, I spilled onto the beach barefoot and topless with just one thing on my mind.

To face the ocean.

Like Vivian had.

I wouldn't go far, I convinced myself. I only wanted to wade in and trust her again. Trust her riptides wouldn't swallow me. Trust her waves would carry me back to shore each time. The ocean was the OG, the original gangster, the biggest source of my fears, and I needed to conquer her.

I waded out two feet, warm salty water up to my knees, and closed my eyes. I thought of poor Vivian doing the same ninety years ago, walking into the ocean with a broken heart, letting it squelch her pain by consuming her. I only wanted to make peace.

"Mother Ocean, heal my broken heart. Wash away the pain. Lull me in your soft waves. As above the surface, so below." I used Jeanine's words in my own way, to remind myself there was peace above the horizon as well as below it.

Employing every cell of trust I ever had, I leaned back and lifted my feet to the water line, then floated like I had with Diego, holding air deep in my lungs, arms out wide. I kept my eye on the full moon for focus and guidance. I was doing great. Nothing to worry about.

See? It's just water.

As if conquering my fears wasn't enough, something moved underneath me. Before I could react or allow panic to control me, I told myself to listen, feel, recognize... *You know this sensation. You know what it is.* Yes, I did. I'd first felt that touch of softness many moons ago, felt the familiar bump of hard nose against my body, felt the playful nudge of curiosity against my side when I was just a toddler, succumbing to the ocean's pull. I kept my breath calm, palms face down in the water, so I could feel smooth, rubbery skin brush up against my fingers.

Feel her rubbery skin.

Yes, her—I knew in my heart it was a "she," this sweet, maternal creature swimming by in the night, nudging my floating body to make sure I was okay. I knew in my soul the dolphin was a mother like me, trying to lift another one up. Could it be Vivian? Had she been the one to find me so many years ago? Saved my life then, and now again in a new way? Heartbroken, wandering the ocean forever, visiting her old haunt to make sure her home and its new residents were okay?

From one childless mother to another, I understood. And appreciated her checking on me.

twenty-one

A FAT, ripe orange-and-red mango sat on the porch, bobbling back and forth in the strong wind. Mono would love that, but so would I. Entering the kitchen with the fruit, I sliced off both sides around the seed, then returned to the porch and dropped one of the pieces into Mono's bowl.

"Enjoy," I told him, wherever he was.

Locking up, I enjoyed a sense of peace unlike anything I'd felt in recent days. Months. Years. Whether the moon party or the night swim was responsible, I wasn't sure. I ate the other half of mango while walking down Mango Road on my way to work, noticing the extra barricades and security guards who'd been hired this week ever since the ghosthunter incident.

When I arrived, through the front this time now that they'd finished taping, I was surprised to see Lily on the porch so early, along with Jax and Rick, the other guard.

"Good morning," I greeted, heading up the steps.

"Reggie." Lily stopped me. "Do you have a moment?"

Uh, oh, more questions.

"I know you've been asked this already by the police, but do you remember at all who was at Montero House the other night?"

"Besides the ghost hunters?"

"Yes."

"I don't," I said, "and I don't want to throw anyone under the bus either without being a hundred percent sure."

"I understand," she said. "That's fair."

"Is everything okay?" I asked the group.

Jax removed his captain's hat to scratch his hair. He had nice hair. "It's just we finally got back the video from Mrs. Patisse's security camera, and the improved quality shows it looks like one of them might be—"

Lily cut him off with a look.

"One of our own," Jax finished.

"I didn't even know Mrs. Patisse had a security camera. That's great! I mean, bad that it might be one of our own." I tried to sound sympathetic.

"Thanks, Reg. I'll call you if I need anything else." Lily turned back to Rick and Jax, while I entered the house, noticing Josephine and Callie standing by the front window eavesdropping. I stood with them, pretending to rearrange coffee cups on the dining room cupboard so the chefs in the kitchen wouldn't think I was being nosy.

A minute later, Maya sauntered into the house through the back, set her bag on a couch (which we weren't allowed to do) like she lived there, and marched toward the front door, giving me a sharp eye. I ducked into the corner next to the massive armoire. Through the open window, I could just barely hear them.

"You called me, Ms. Lily?" Maya asked.

From her sigh, I could tell that Lily was uncomfortable. "Honey, I hate to ask you this, but do you have any idea how those people got into Montero House the other night? From our reports, the doors were locked, you told the police you were staying with your friends in Key Largo, and Regina was not home."

There was muttering, but I couldn't hear. Maya was keeping her voice low for the first time in Maya history. Even the chefs were pressing their ears to the windows. The first guest of the morning clomped downstairs, a zombie in search of coffee.

"Good morning. Right here," I said, showing them where to find it, then shifted closer to the window.

"I don't," Maya said. "I only know they investigate haunted and abandoned places."

"So, you don't know who let them in?"

"No clue," Maya replied. I let out a sigh of relief. I wasn't sure why I was glad she wasn't involved. "I only know that I watch their videos, and in the last one, they said they were going to investigate Montero House because of its reputation."

"Because it's haunted," Rick clarified, as if we didn't already know.

"Yes, but also because there's treasure there, supposedly," Maya said.

My ears strained to listen.

"There's treasure all over the Keys," Lily muttered. "The hope of finding some is what brings so many people here."

"Doesn't help that we found some ourselves recently," Jax added.

"What they said in their video—"

"The ghosthunters?" Lily interrupted.

"Yes, the *Ghost Crew*, the YouTubers, is that the lady who lived there a long time ago used to hide her money in the house because she didn't trust the banks."

Jax chimed in. "That was pretty common in Prohibition days."

"Right, and because the house is under construction, they thought it would be a good time to look for it," Lily said with a sigh. "I got it."

"But we still need to know who let them in," Jax said.

"Maybe Regina didn't lock up when she left," Maya said. "Or one of the construction workers."

Or maybe you, I thought. *Or Serge was bribed to let them through.*

"I mean, it's possible Regina invited them over. You know how creepy she is. Several of us saw her take a Ouija board from your house, too, Ms. Lily."

What? My blood boiled. The chefs craned their necks to stare at me. *No, I'm sorry.* I charged over and yanked open the door. "That is not true. You can ask Diego. I was with him."

Maya's face fell when she saw I'd been listening in.

"Diego says you were with him, but then you left," Rick said to me.

"I left because I got a bad feeling that something was going on. And I was right. I arrived to find people in the house, but I'm not the one who let them in." I implored Lily. "I wouldn't do that to you. You can check Mrs. Patisse's video."

Maya's face went cold—she obviously hadn't realized a video was involved. Lily gave me a slow blink that said I had nothing to worry about. But it still pissed me off that this girl had the balls to throw me under the bus, especially after I'd done my best to be fair to her. Well, not anymore.

"She's an actress," I blurted. "It's the only reason she's here, to try to land a spot as your next show's host. She's not even a housekeeper, which is an insult to actual housekeepers."

Maya inhaled sharply and stared at me with eye daggers. "*You're* an insult to housekeepers."

Oof, this girl.

"Is that true?" Lily looked from me to Maya.

I walked off but then stopped at the door. "Lily, you already knew about me taking the Ouija board. I told you myself. And while I wasn't sure before and still am not sure now, I'm at least eighty percent sure I heard Maya's voice with the ghosthunters that night. I didn't want to accuse you before," I told Maya, "but now I don't care."

Jax finally pulled out the pièce de résistance, the improved quality video on his phone. "Is this you?" He turned the phone around to face Maya.

She crossed her arms and blew out a slow breath.

"Alright," Lily said, arms flapping against her sides. "Go pack. Your last check will be direct deposited."

"What about Regina?" Maya gaped.

"She's fired, too," Lily said.

My heart dropped, mouth hung open. *What did I...*

"And rehired," Lily added without missing a beat. Jax hid his smile in his shoulder. "Like I said, go pack."

Maya stormed into the house, whizzing past me like a Category 5 storm. Lily leaned into Jax for a side hug. "I hate firing people."

"I know." He kissed the top of her head.

I tried to sneak away.

"Reggie?"

"Ma'am?" I reappeared in the doorway.

"I knew it wasn't you, just for the record. Maya's been a guest on those boys' videos several times in the past. We just wanted her to admit it before we busted her."

"Thank you." I nodded and went back to work, proud of my job and of myself. But something was still bothering me, and I could not for the life of me figure out what it was.

As I walked home that evening, exhausted, physically and mentally, from all the drama, I tried to put clarity to mind to figure out what I was feeling. Tired? Check. Angry at Maya? Check. Appreciated by my employer? Check. Still, something niggled at me, and it wasn't until I saw a business card lying on the ground with the name *Second Treasures* that I knew...

Maya had said there was treasure in the house.

Any treasure would certainly belong to Lily Autumn, but where had I heard this before? I didn't watch those ghosthunters' channel, so it couldn't be there, and I hadn't read up on history of Skeleton Key before taking this job like Lily and the others had, so it couldn't be that. Had Diego mentioned it, or maybe one of the ghosts had during the séances?

When I arrived on my street just in time to see the construction trucks whisking rubble away, I noticed the broken, mangled remnants of marble and rock. The fireplace, the one I loved to run my hand on to feel its smoothness. Sad that they had to demolish it, but it had been in rather bad shape, and it was time for renewal.

The truck stopped at the stop sign.

I stopped on the sidewalk.

Notes in the fireplace, Vivian's voice from my last dream with her echoed through time. *Have it.*

Notes in the fireplace.

Weren't "notes" another word for money, as in bank notes? Dollar bills?

The truck lunged forward with a roar.

"Wait!" I cried. "Waiiiit!" I ran toward the truck, my purse slapping against my side, but the driver couldn't hear me. Luckily, he had two more stop signs before reaching Overseas Highway, and I was in good shape.

I ran my hardest toward the truck. "Stoooop!" Out of breath, I reached the back of the vehicle and slammed my hand on the metal siding to make a loud bang. The driver's face appeared in the sideview mirror. He stuck his head out the open window.

"Can I check this...before...before you take it?" I wheezed out my request. I could be totally wrong, but it wouldn't hurt to check the fireplace before I never saw it again.

The truck jolted into Park and the driver hopped out. "You lose something?"

"Maybe." I climbed the side of the truck, placed one leg inside the bed, one leg out, straddling the edge to keep from losing my balance. "I need to check this fireplace." It was in pieces. Complete rubble, along with a few big chunks of rock. I wasn't even sure what I was looking for, only that I remembered Vivian telling me I could keep "the notes in the fireplace." As I did after most dreams, I'd forgotten the details.

I looked underneath the mantlepiece, behind the rock pieces, and everywhere around the broken debris. No notes, or bills, or anything to do with money. "Is there more to this?"

The driver tipped his chin in the direction of the house. "Whatever else is left would be over there."

"Okay, thanks. Sorry I yelled at you."

He chuckled. "No worries."

I accepted his hand in helping me down, smoothed back my hair, and adjusted my purse strap. Then, once he drove off, I broke into a sprint again without slowing until I made it to the house. There, I stumbled onto the porch, past Mono's empty food dish, the capuchin himself gnawing on a piece of fruit, and into the great room of the Montero House.

A few workers were still cleaning up, hauling away debris. Where the fireplace once stood was now a gaping rectangle, which a worker was trying to smooth out the jagged edges of drywall with a sharp-edged tool. One of the ghosthunters had talked about checking inside the fireplace. It was the last thing they talked about before I scared them away.

"Excuse me," I called, stepping over a pile of rubble and past the dusty-faced worker. "Can I look in there real quick?"

"Be my guest." He set his tool down on the floor, wiped his brow, and walked outside, leaving me alone with the fireplace and Mono by my side.

First, I crouched, then ducked my head into the space between the walls. What was I looking for? Even if Vivian had left money in there, what would old, decrepit cash be worth now? Like twenty bucks? Running my hands between the sheets of gypsum board, I cringed at the possibility of breathing in cancerous asbestos from these outdated materials.

Nothing.

Then, I noticed a brick behind the spot where the fireplace had been. Brick underneath drywall that'd been partially torn out. Someone had decided they hated the look of exposed brick and covered it up with the stuff, the edges of which were getting ripped up anyway, so I pried my fingers underneath and took out more pieces, then more pieces, exposing more and more of the brick wall underneath.

Mono was trying to do the same at the bottom to no avail.

"That's tomorrow's task." The man was back, hands on his hips. "Careful. You'll destroy your nails that way."

"I clean toilets for a living. I'm okay with it," I said, continuing to madly tear more and more pieces away with my bare hands.

"Let me help you." He circled around with the tool, which had a crowbar on the opposite end, jammed it underneath the drywall, and pried off large chunks at a time. "If it were my house, I'd refurbish this brick. It's actually really nice," he said between grunts.

We tore off the drywall within three feet of the fireplace but still, there were no bills or anything that looked like money, and the men were leaving. My helper dusted off his tool, set it against the wall. "Maybe tomorrow, we'll put you on the payroll, huh?" He laughed and headed out.

As the house emptied, all I could do was stare at the wall, while Mono chirped at my feet. A brick wall and an opening for the fireplace flue. Whatever was once there was no longer. Once again, it appeared that Vivian had spoken to me from her era, without seeming to understand that things had changed since she'd lived.

There were no notes. No treasure.

"Thanks, anyway." I placed my hand on the wall. Then, I saw it—one brick.

One brick set slightly deeper into the wall than the rest and didn't have the same thickness of grout or concrete around it as the others. I leaned into it, or maybe it leaned out to me, same as the fireplace mantle had every time I walked past it with the urge to run my hands along it. The brick was set too far inside for me to grab its outer edges, so I reached for the worker's tool and wedged the sharp edge into the loose space, hoping to pry it out.

It barely moved. The edge was too blunt, not thin enough to force out a brick, so I ran to the kitchen and nearly died laughing when I saw Mono sitting atop the counter, trying to cut another mango with the knife I'd used this morning. He handed it to me and chirped.

"Yes, thank you!" I took it.

A thin knife would fit nicely in that slim space. For that moment, I imagined that I was Vivian, moving some painting she might've had atop her fireplace mantle long ago, using any old kitchen knife to pry out a brick. A daily routine that she did to store the day's earnings or pull out a bill or two to pay workers. Just one brick.

Little by little, the brick slid out, and I carefully set it on the floor. The space wheezed a sigh. Inside was narrow but deep and filled, stuffed to the brim like a Thanksgiving turkey, except instead of carrots and celery, there was cash, lots of it—thick, old, humid, stained rolls of dollar bills. Judging from how many were taking up space at just the front of the makeshift deposit box, there had to be at least fifty thick wads of cash, and each one had—I pulled out to inspect—20-dollar notes, 50-dollar notes, 100-dollar notes.

There had to be thousands of dollars in here.

If Vivian didn't trust banks, this had to be her entire savings. But without her husband and daughter to share it with, she'd stepped outside in heartache, walked into the ocean, and left it all behind. Here. In this house.

twenty-two

WE WERE ON THE OCEAN—LILY, Heloise, Sid, Katja, Evan, Jeanine, Sam, a new friend of Sam's, Jax, and I— on Captain Jax's beautiful charter boat, headed to Key West on a sparklingly gorgeous Labor Day. For once, it was not a dream, and for once, I was not riddled with anxiety.

Six months had passed since the day I found the famous cigar factory owner Vivian Montero's bankroll. Six months since I showed Lily what I'd discovered on her property, and six months since she told me we would split it 50/50, no matter what the appraisal value came back to be.

I was flabbergasted. She could've kept it all to herself or offered a nominal finder's fee of 15%, but no—that was not who Lily Autumn was. "I wouldn't even have it if it weren't for you, Reg," she'd said. "Fifty-fifty is fair."

With loads of guilt and mixed emotions, I accepted the offer. "I bet the previous owners who sold you the house are kicking themselves in the butt right about now, huh?"

Paper money pre-dating the 1940s, as it turned out, was very valuable, but the currency would need to go through a series of carbon-testing procedures before we'd know for sure just how much. In the meantime, I kept working at *House of Dolls*. Housekeeping was what I did, though Lily began paying me to create schedules, assign duties, and manage the other workers, some of which were now men, because Lily had listened to my wish that stereotypes and stigma in housekeeping might one day be broken. I'd never been Manager of Housekeeping before. Felt like a step in the right direction.

The only thing missing from this boat trip was Diego. As luck would have it, he had to labor on Labor Day, working in Marathon Key all morning. The plan was to meet sometime tomorrow at Montero House then go back to his place, a great idea so I could spend more time with my friends.

I never imagined I'd be on a glistening white boat, sipping mojitos crafted by Salty Sid, catching cool ocean spray on a blistering hot day. I never imagined I'd be on the ocean ever again, and to be honest, I wasn't completely okay. I was the only one not whooping it up, taking selfies, or dancing to ABBA tunes on the bow. Instead, I sat near Captain Jax in the shade where it felt safer.

"Are you okay? I know boating's not your thing. Sorry if we forced you to come." Jax piloted with one foot up on a stool, his nimble shaded eyes on the horizon.

"I wasn't forced." I moved my gaze to the shoreline. "Not by you all, anyway. By me. I've been pushing myself out of my comfort zone lately. Doing the inner work. It's amazing how much you grow when you do that."

"I hear you. I'd never be where I am now if I hadn't done the same. I'd still be whining about not having much business, clients being unable to find me, wondering why I couldn't pay bills."

I nodded slowly. "Yep."

Island after island of beautiful waterfront homes, and I'd never, ever stop wondering what each of those homeowners did for a living. Except, instead of imagining faceless, callous millionaires, I now imagined cooks, bakers, celebrity chefs, bed-and-breakfast owners, dollmakers, ice cream vendors, eco adventure CEOs, kind, generous people who shared their wealth in many different ways.

"I'm not merely paying bills for the first time in my life," I said. "I'm actually saving a bit."

"Thriving, not just surviving, huh?" Jax said.

"Exactly." I'd even looked into a small house in Miami near Andreas' apartment, but the prices were outrageous, and I wasn't there yet. Banks wanted to see more stability before they approved you for a loan. "I couldn't have done it without Lily. Without all you guys. What a band of moral supporters you are, my goodness."

He laughed. "It takes a village."

"It sure does."

"Another mojito?" Salty Sid came around with his tray of handmade concoctions, this one peachy in color. "Mango mojitos from your front yard." He laughed.

Ah, so that was where they'd gone. Mono and I had gone through the last of the season, but I could've sworn there'd been a few left on the tree. "Sure, why not?" I took a frosty glass off his tray and sipped. "Mmmm. Good."

There was an older woman on this boat I'd never seen before and hadn't seen come onboard either. She smiled and stared a lot at Jax. "Did your mom love the ocean?" I asked him.

"My mom? She adored it, yeah. An ocean goddess."

The woman wore a seashell on a chain around her neck. "A sea witch," I said. I didn't mind using the word witch to describe anyone anymore. It felt honest, natural, and true.

"Have I told you about her?" Jax squinted at me curiously.

"No. But she's here with us now. I knew it was your mom because she can't stop staring at you." I sipped my mojito.

Jax was silent. Then, after a moment. "Is she proud of me?"

"So proud of you. So, so proud," I replied. It was true. The woman could not stop beaming.

And that was really all people ever wanted from the spirit world, was to know that their loved ones were happy on the other side, that they were proud of their efforts, that they were no longer in anguish or pain.

When we reached Key West, I was happy to step on land, but my soul wanted to split open. This was it—the southern-most city in the United States, the last stop before the Florida Straits, 90 miles to Havana. In all my years living in this country, I'd never been this close to my home island again, and my heart ached all over again.

"You okay, love?" Heloise asked as we walked to the famous buoy marking the spot. I'd seen it a million times in photos. Never thought I'd see it in person.

"I'll be okay."

She held my hand, just in case.

When we arrived, we stood in line, took photos, then stood next to the seawall staring out south to sea. She was out there, my beautiful homeland, my paradise lost, a place I'd never go again.

"Will you ever go back?" Sid whispered beside me.

I shook my head. "Not until things change. The money we spend there goes straight into the wrong pockets. The people get nothing. I can't support that, Sid."

He nodded. "I get that, kid. I get it."

As I stood there looking out to sea, to the straits where my parents risked death to bring me to safety, I felt the reverent silence of my friends, as they stood by. *Te quiero mucho, Mami y Papi.* I wiped my eyes and took a deep breath. When I was done wallowing, I remembered my blessings and thanked the universe for my life. I thought perhaps everyone was waiting for me to say something profound, but all I could think to say was, "I'm hungry. Anyone else hungry?"

"Yes!" They laughed.

"Let's grab some food!" Lily announced, then led the way across the street to an oceanside café with outdoor seating under thatched roof and ceiling fans.

There, we settled into several tables pushed together, and I had a moment of déjà vu. Even though I'd never met any of these people before February, I felt like we'd all done this before, like we'd been gathering and celebrating life forever, and that was something I'd never felt with the family that raised me. Had I been making my way to them all my life?

After we ordered food and drinks, everyone broke into smaller chats, and Lily turned to me. In her eyes, I saw the usual kindness but something more—she had information. I tried my best not to extract it from her mind through psychic means and just let her tell me.

"The appraisal came back," she said.

"And it's more than you thought," I said.

"And it's more than I thought," she acknowledged.

"Some of the hundreds are worth $200-400 more per bill," I guessed. I couldn't help it.

"Who's telling who here?"

"Sorry. You go."

"Some of the hundreds are worth $200-600 *more* per bill," she corrected, proud of the fact that she had better information than what my third eye could pick up. "Some were greenbacks, some gold certificate, some silver, some from the 1920s, some from the 1930s, some in better shape than others." She paused for a breath. "Which brings the entire amount that was worth—"

"$3,533 in Vivian's time..." I reminded her.

"Correct...to $3,112,552 today."

I stared at her. Her eyes were mossy green.

She was beautiful, not just for her age, but in general. All around was chatter, seagulls cawing, children laughing on the beach, music playing, ocean waves crashing against the dock. But I wasn't sure what she said. "What was that?"

"You heard me. $3,112,552."

"In dollars?"

She sniffed a laugh. "Yes. How does that feel?"

"I've never had more than a few hundred dollars in my bank account at any given time, Lily. How does it feel? Surreal. This isn't happening."

"But it is. Aren't you happy?" she asked.

"Of course," I replied. Wasn't that the correct way to react? Then, why couldn't I feel it?

I was holding back, reserving my enthusiasm, in part because I couldn't believe it. That kind of money did not belong to me. It never had and never would. But that was Daniel talking. The truth was, it had never belonged to other people before their luck either. So, I was holding back for other reasons—fear again. What if it was a mistake? What if something came along and swiped this out from under my nose? Good things didn't stay good for long.

"Nothing bad is going to happen, Regina," she told me. "Everything bad that will ever happen to you has *already* happened. Do you hear me?"

I nodded.

"You've already paid your dues," she said. "Now you collect. That's how the universe works. There is balance."

I was the proud new owner of $1,556,276? Half the sum?

"Now comes the chapter in your life where everything goes smoothly," Lily continued on in my stunned silence. "The money flows, the love flows, the joy, the abundance, the gratitude...all of it. Don't doubt it. It happened to me—all of us—it can happen to you, too. Do you believe me?"

"I do," I said. And I did.

"There's more."

"You're going to kill me."

I could already see it, like a ticker tape parade in her eyes, the words making themselves known to me before she could speak them. "Diego and I have been talking."

Diego? I hadn't seen him in four days because of business meetings, and I sorely missed him. After dating for six months, a girl got used to being spoiled. So did a monkey with an ice cream addiction.

"He's been busy," I said.

Lily nodded. "That's because we're talking business. The house is almost finished," she continued.

Don't ask me to host a show, don't ask me to host a show...

"And Diego approached me, asked if he could open an ice cream shop at *Dead & Breakfast*. Sales have been great with his kiosk."

"At one of the guest houses?"

"On the boardwalk."

"Boardwalk?" Now, I was confused.

She smiled. "We're going half on a boardwalk, Reg. Isn't that exciting? He's a longtime resident of Islamorada, has history with people in the area, you know."

"Yes, his great-grandfather worked for Vivian Montero."

"Right. He has just as much a stake in wanting to see *Dead & Breakfast* grow and expand. And so, we're going to build the boardwalk that Vivian lost, connect the three *Dead & Breakfast* houses together."

I stared at her in a daze. My God, could Vivian hear this? Where was a ghost when you needed her?

Heloise leaned in from the other side. "Are we talking about the boardwalk? Did you tell her about the crystal shop?"

Lily swatted Heloise's face with a napkin. "Excuse me, we're in an important business meeting here. Eat some conch fritters."

"I'm out." Heloise's face retreated.

"As I was saying..." Lily straightened to face me more head-on. "He wants to see the boardwalk that Annie,

Josephine, and Vivian, even Sylvie all wanted to come to fruition. It's time to make that happen."

"I love this so much," I finally spoke.

"Me, too. We're giving Jax a kiosk there for his charter boat business, Diego will get an ice cream store on the new boardwalk, because that boy is obsessed, I tell you, and to go with the ghost theme at Montero House, we want a Ouija board shop."

"A Ouija board shop?"

"A metaphysical store. A new age boutique. You know, a 'crystal shop,' as Weezy said. At first, I was just going to ask if you'd run the store for me. But then, the appraisal news came in. Now, I'm not going to tell you what to do with your newly-earned money, but I would love it if you and I went half on the shop. I want to see you holding readings, performing séances, helping people reach their loved ones."

"This can't be happening."

"It is, if you want it to. Like I said, you're free to go anytime you want. I know you never liked coming to the Keys. I know it reminds you of Cuba. I know you've been counting the days until you can buy a house somewhere north." Lily looked at me. "But just consider?"

Where would I live?

"You can stay at Montero House on the days you're not sleeping at Diego's." She turned to high-five Heloise who was still eavesdropping. "Or not, I don't care. But you have a room there, if you want it, if it makes your life easier."

"Did you just...read my mind?" I asked.

"Two can play that game, Reg."

"Take the deal, Serra!" Jeanine shouted across the table. Seemed everyone was listening. "To think we almost sold our home to Atlantis Cruise Line. None of this would be happening. Take it, girl. She hasn't offered us shit!"

"Shh." Lily batted Jeanine away.

"You won't put me on TV, right?" I whispered.

"Of all things, this is what you worry about?" Lily dropped her chin and laughed. "Oh, Reg. No, I haven't gotten a deal with the networks yet. We're still waiting on ratings for Season 2, so you don't have to worry about being on TV. But what do you think about the shop? You said you always wanted to own one, remember?"

I did remember. "I remember telling you I didn't care what kind. Way to aim high!" I shook my head.

Lily had a lovely faraway look on her face. "Seems so long ago, doesn't it? Life changes from one day to the next. So much has changed since I decided to stay here. Anyway, think about it. I won't be offended if you still want to leave, but you're the first person I wanted to share a shop with and the perfect person to run it, too. Assuming you'd want to. Anyway, food's here."

The magic of our moment melted, as she twisted in her seat and faced the rest of our party, sharing the various appetizers and dishes she'd ordered with anyone who wanted to try.

I pretended to be absorbed by my salmon with citrus-lime crema and guava coleslaw, but my mind was spinning its wheels. Yes, it'd been painful coming here, a slap to the face, but that was only because I couldn't see the whole picture. All along, the universe had been plotting, pieces of a larger puzzle falling into place without my knowing, and healing had begun. Healing—near the place where the pain began.

Though none of it would've been possible without a change in me. I could credit Lily, Diego, Sid, Heloise, Katja, Vivian, and all the other lovely people and spirits who helped guide me until the cows came home, but until I made the change in myself, none of it would've happened.

"What did I miss?" A deep, sexy voice joined the chorus of chatter. I turned to see Diego joining us at the café, looking good enough to eat in his island shirt, and hat. He even held a cigar in his pocket, which he quickly offered to Sid. "For you, my friend."

"Hey, hey, thanks!"

"The mogul made it!" Katja looked at me and gave me a sly wink.

I wasn't halfway out of my chair to green him before Diego scooped me into his arms and laid a huge kiss on me. I probably blushed eight different shades of red. I'd never been kissed so passionately with so many people watching before. "And these," he handed me a cluster of tangerine roses, "are for you."

I took the roses amid a collective "aww" from our party. "Thank you. I missed you."

"Missed you more." He squeezed into a chair, and I looked around at my current life.

No, I didn't want to leave. I wanted to stay in Skeleton Key with all its weirdness, ghosts, and history. I wanted to live in "haunted" Montero House, and I wanted to help people with private readings inside my own shop. Most of all, I wanted to stay with the new love I'd found and with my friends.

I looked at them all, the witches and protectors of Skeleton Key. Giving them up would be a mistake. I never wanted to be a part of something so wonderful more in all my life.

"Lily." I leaned into her.

"What's up?"

"Yes."

"Yes?" Her eyebrows rose.

"Yes." I smiled. I couldn't help it, the tears came. Of course, they did.

"Come here." Lily stood, and I stood, chairs scraping along the wooden decking, and with everyone watching, my boss and witchy friend hugged me hard and lifted my arm in the air. "Everybody, she's in!"

The table erupted into cheers.

twenty-three

I WAS DREAMING AGAIN.

Not drowning, not swimming, not panicking, no angels nudging me upwards in the water. I stood on a beach looking out to shore, waiting for someone to arrive. I wore a beautiful yellow dress, radiant as the sun. All along the beach were the residents of Skeleton Key, gussied up as well. The real sun in the sky above was cool, brilliant and lovely. Its light contained all the love this world could hold.

My stomach fluttered with excitement. Today was the day—the day everything would change. The first day of the rest of my life. A new chapter, as Lily had said at the café that day almost a year ago.

In the distance, a speck appeared, one that grew larger and larger the closer it got, as it took its time. It wouldn't be hurried, and I understood that it might not even arrive today. Whatever it was, possibly a raft, it might not wash up on the beach for another several months or years, because some things were not to be rushed.

And so, I waited.

Time moved slowly, if at all, but eventually, the speck was close enough for me to see it wasn't a raft at all but a boat, gleaming white and navy, sparkling clean and bright— a luxurious superyacht carrying many people waving on the front bow.

Excitedly, I waved, because although I didn't know who they were, I felt, in this very lucid dream, that they were somehow important. They'd traveled from far away to deliver something I'd ordered long ago, a shipment that got lost along the way that had finally been found. A whole ship just to deliver my goods!

The closer it got, the more I could see the faces of those who greeted me—smiling, happy faces of people I'd never seen before in my life but who, at the same time, felt familiar. A horn blew a loud, vibrating honk, signaling that the wait had ended, and then, a lifeboat was lowered on the side of the ship, and a little motor turned on. My friends gathered closer, as we waited to welcome the new guests to our party.

I didn't recognize these folks, either, except I did, all of a sudden, after a moment of studying them. *Mami? Papi?* My parents—my mother and father—only older, grayer, wearing finer threads than anything they could afford in the short life I remembered them. At times, Daniel was there, too, lingering in the periphery, unsure if he should approach. At times, he faded, but I knew he was there. I couldn't hear voices as we might speak them aloud, but they greeted me just the same in their own, silent dream language. I hugged them in one fell swoop, ringing my arms around both sets of shoulders.

I've missed you guys. Thank you. Thank you for my life, I told them.

My mother smiled her shining eyes into mine, and my father tousled my hair, and then they separated, and someone else stepped out of the boat, swishing his feet through the water until he reached the shore. He was bare-foot, wore jeans and a fine buttoned-down shirt rolled up at the sleeves, his hair swept to the side, and his face was that of a happy-go-lucky kid.

Pablito.

He was real, here with me! A visit—finally—a real-life visit in the astral world. This was why the islanders had gathered, to come and meet my family, even Daniel. If I thought I was dreaming, all logic was challenged the moment my son approached me and lowered his face, so I could see deeply into his brown eyes and know that he was real, his gaze deeper than I could ever see into anyone here on Earth. Two souls reunited.

Hi, Mom.

Mi amor. I threw my arms around him and smiled into his shoulder, radiating all the love in my heart, more energy than the rays of the sun above us. *You finally came. What took so long?*

I got caught up.

We laughed.

I want you to meet everyone. I've told them so much about you. Bubbles of pride rose, danced, and sparkled inside my chest, as Pablito walked around shaking hands of everyone on the beach. I introduced them one by one—Lily, Diego, Sid, Katja—the whole crew. He told stories of how far he'd come, how much he was like me, how his father was a good man, too, who should never be forgotten.

I looked at Daniel who dipped his head.

I smiled at him.

We walked toward the Montero House, now finished. The party would take place outside in the wraparound veranda. In a few minutes, we'd feast, drink, dance to lively music, tell stories...except when my feet actually touched the house, I could tell the visitors weren't by my side anymore. I turned, beckoning them to come closer, but they stood where the water met the sand.

Come! Come inside, I called. They couldn't leave now. They'd just gotten here! I wanted, needed more time with them, but they waved to me from a distance, and I knew they weren't joining us to stay.

They couldn't go where I was going.

That didn't mean, however, that they couldn't visit from time to time.

The sun filled the whole sky. It grew so bright, I couldn't see anyone anymore. All I could feel was Pablito's hug tight around me and his kiss on my forehead. The smell of plumeria permeated the air. Love, greater than the sun, wider than all the universe, filled up my room. My room?

My eyes fluttered opened.

I took in my beautiful apartment at the old Montero House, a new addition built in the back with the boardwalk leading right up to it. The early morning sunlight streamed in, hitting the white walls, white bedspread, and new furniture. On the nightstand next to me were flowers—plumeria. I hadn't seen these in a year. In fact, after scouring the whole east side of the island with Diego one day, we couldn't find a single plumeria tree.

Had my son been the one leaving them all along?

I lifted them to my nose and hugged the fragile blooms to

my chest. "You were here," I muttered then broke into a smile. "You were here."

It wasn't the only thing on my nightstand. There, steaming from one of the new porcelain cups designed specifically for the new *Dead & Breakfast* opening today was a cup of coffee, lots of cream, lots of sugar, a pinch of cinnamon floating on top.

"Are you kidding me?" With shaking hands, I took it, kept it steady all the way to my lips, and with tears falling into my coffee, drank my first sip in years.

Montero House reopened at 2 PM, aptly called *Spirit Boardwalk Dead & Breakfast*, but I wasn't the manager of the establishment. One had yet to be hired. Instead, I was part owner and manager of the new age witch shop in the old cigar room downstairs, the one filled with witchy accoutrements, glass spheres, crystals in every shape, size, and color, tarot cards, packaged herbs, spell books and grimoires, pendulums, and all the necessary items to pull off magickal feats of manifestation, and of course, a fine collection of hand-crafted spirit boards.

In the back room was a yoga studio where a young lady prepared to give her first class, and next to that was a private room. On the wall of this reading chamber was Sylvie Collier's spirit board and planchette, the reading table was made of the wood of a raft that had safely brought twenty-two people from Cuba to Key West twenty years before. It felt wonderfully charged with positive, hopeful energy. Three chairs were from Vivian's cigar factory, items procured by Diego during an auction this summer. But my favorite piece, by far, was the large, gorgeous mirror on the wall behind my chair in the shape of a dolphin covered in tiny silver, aquamarine, and green crystals. It'd been commissioned by Lily from a local artist as a gift to me.

In the corner on the floor was a pillow bed for Mono to sleep on whenever his little monkey brain needed a nap (like now—the fuzzbutt was curled up on it), and next to it was a small, silver wastebin with a swinging door so he could properly dispose of ice cream cups. A special room indeed.

The rest of the bed-and-breakfast had been given a ghostly Victorian theme, with framed photos of vintage spirit photography, some with ectoplasm coming out of their noses, some with dead family members lingering in the backgrounds, and a whole hallway with the best alleged photos of ghosts ever taken. But my favorite had to be the apothe"scary" guest bathroom downstairs, complete with floral light covers, real chemist bottles, absinthe bottles, and paraphernalia from the 1890s, and jars full of oddities and curiosities.

"Regina!" Someone was calling from inside the adjacent house. Kevin, our director.

I checked my appearance in the mirror—gauzy gray dress with fringe knotted at my slim waist, one toned thigh sticking out the slit, my long hair in sexy waves over one shoulder. Makeup? On point, with cat-wing eyeliner carefully applied by one Katja Miller, and on my outer right eye was a tiny moon crystal.

"Ms. Serra on the set!" Kevin called again.

"Coming!" I shuffled through the private reading room, through the store, lightly touching every other item with my newly manicured nails.

Outside the door to the shop were cameras, lights, rigs, microphones, assistant grips, grips, Lily, Heloise, Kevin, Sid, and everyone else who ever loved this little island. I stood on my taped X mark.

"*Coñó, mira quien está aquí. La reina de mi corazón,*" a sexy voice spoke in my ear, as a strong forearm wrapped around my waist. Diego frequently passed by my shop on his way to *The Sweet Spot* next door. "Queen of my heart. You know that's what your name means, right?"

"Of course, I do," I purred, running my fingertip along his stubbled beard. "You weren't the first man to love me."

"I'll be your last." He kissed my cheek, sending too many shivers up my spine.

"Get a room." From somewhere in the back, Sid's voice rang out. I searched for him. Was that a lobster he was holding? He whistled one of his little songs until Kevin asked him to be quiet on the set, and he walked off, still holding a lobster. This was my life.

My son Andreas would not be making it today. I'd hoped he would come, but like always, he had an excuse, except today's was a good one—he and my daughter-in-law, Melinda, were having their first ultrasound. That's right, I was a going to be a sexy-ass grandma, and my grandchild would be the first in the family to have a savings account with actual funds in it before he or she was born.

But guess who was here instead?

A happy-go-lucky young man, a dreamer, a kid who loved to wear comic hero T-shirts, a piece of my heart that would never leave me. I waved to Pablito standing in the back near Diego's shop on the boardwalk, as several people glanced behind to see who I'd waved to.

I love you, mi amor.

"Places, everyone," Kevin ordered.

There was a shuffle of movement and a blur of womanly shape who ran past me in a flowing caftan thing and bouncy earrings, blowing kisses in the air. "Good luck!"

"Thanks, Lily. I owe you." I'd said this to her every day since finding the cash stash. I would never stop being grateful.

"Owe you more."

I breathed deeply, letting out the breath in a steady stream. "I can do this, I can do this," I whispered. Who on Earth would've thought I'd be standing here doing the very thing that had terrified me a year ago? Not me. But things changed. Life changed. For the better.

"Quiet on the set," Kevin said through his megaphone. "Just like we rehearsed. Ready? On three...two..." The one was silent.

"Hello, I'm Regina Serra, proud owner of *Spirit Boardwalk Boo-tique* here in beautiful Skeleton Key, and..." I never thought I'd say this. Pointing to the hand-painted sign above me, I delivered the line flawlessly. "We are now OPEN for business!"

next in series

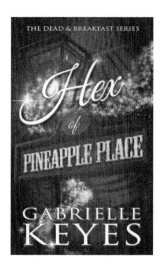

Since being crowned Miss Georgia in 2000, Nikki Lewison has gone nowhere but down. After finding the courage to leave her pastor husband (who only wanted a trophy wife), Nikki has been alone for the last fifteen years. Now that her mother has called her a "lonely old spinster," she's not sure she will ever love again.

When *Dead & Breakfast* owner, Lily Autumn, hires Nikki for some social media marketing, she surprises her with a room-and-board offer in the Florida Keys. And since Nikki can barely afford her Atlanta town-house anymore, she accepts, ready for new adventure.

The last thing she expects to find waiting for her on Skeleton Key is an old Edwardian home. With its turn-of-the-century interiors, bordello-like rooms, and disembodied moans in the middle of the night, creeped-out Nikki is not sure she wants to stay. But the islanders are friendly, her dog Vivaldi loves barking at a mysterious corner of the yard, and the new digs might finally inspire her to excel at the cello.

But can a former beauty queen down on her luck believe in herself again while surrounded by super-successful people? With a host of witchy neighbors intent on helping her access the real Nikki Lewison, she's about to find out.

HEX OF PINEAPPLE PLACE, a Paranormal Women's Fiction novel about starting over in midlife, harnessing the magic within, and friendships after divorce, is Book #4 in the *Dead & Breakfast* series by Gabrielle Keyes.

dear reader...

If you enjoyed this book, please:

- Leave a rating/review on Amazon and Goodreads
- Pre-order Book 4 in the *Dead & Breakfast* Series, HEX OF PINEAPPLE PLACE
- Join my READER GROUP to receive *ONE FREE MAGIC SPELL* each month, new release updates, free chapters, and giveaways.
- Read my other books as GABY TRIANA

Thank you so much for your support!
- *Gabrielle Keyes*

mango ice cream

2 cups ripe mango purée
14 oz. sweetened condensed milk
2 cups heavy cream
3 drops yellow food coloring

1. Dice flesh of 2-3 large, ripe mangos (must be soft and sweet). Purée in a food processor to measure out 2 cups of mango purée.

2. Pour purée into a nonstick skillet over medium heat and

cool, stirring constantly for 8-10 minutes. Reduce by half. Let cool.

3. Combine cooled mango purée and condensed milk in a bowl. Add food coloring if you wish for a more vibrant color. Whisk until combined.

4. Beat cream until stiff peaks form. Scoop a bit of cream and combine with mango mixture. Fold through. Pour mango mixture back into the cream and fold through. Do not mix vigorously.

5. Pour into glass container with lid, placing a piece of parchment paper on surface. Freeze for 12 hours or more.

6. Remove from freezer and let stand 5 minutes before serving.

Enjoy!
Gabrielle Keyes

GABRIELLE KEYES is the Paranormal Women's Fiction pen name of Gaby Triana, bestselling horror author of 21 novels for teens and adults, including the Haunted Florida series (*Island of Bones, River of Ghosts, City of Spells*), *Wake the Hollow, Cakespell, Summer of Yesterday,* and *Paradise Island: A Sam and Colby Story*. She's a short story contributor in *Classic Monsters Unleashed, Weird Tales Magazine* #365, and host of YouTube channel, *The Witch Haunt*.

Published with HarperCollins and Simon & Schuster, Gaby writes about modern witches, ghosts, haunted places, and abandoned locations. She's ghostwritten 50+ novels for bestselling authors, and her books have won IRA Teen Choice, ALA Best Paperback, and Hispanic Magazine's Good Reads Awards. She lives in Miami with her family and a gaggle of four-legged aliens.

also by gabrielle keyes

Dead & Breakfast Series:

WITCH OF KEY LIME LANE

CRONE OF COCONUT COURT

MAGE OF MANGO ROAD

HEX OF PINEAPPLE PLACE

Books as Gaby Triana:

MOON CHILD

PARADISE ISLAND: A SAM & COLBY STORY

ISLAND OF BONES

RIVER OF GHOSTS

CITY OF SPELLS

CAKESPELL

WAKE THE HOLLOW

SUMMER OF YESTERDAY

RIDING THE UNIVERSE

THE TEMPTRESS FOUR

CUBANITA

BACKSTAGE PASS